Allison Leamon had never thought she wanted this kind of romance. There wasn't room in her life for it. It was superficial and fleeting and only fools believed in its authenticity.

Didn't she know better than anyone that sex was mechanical? It was purely biological and physical and had little or nothing to do with the emotions. Any two creatures of the same species could mate. It required nothing of them but properly working reproductive organs.

But here she was, no longer a pragmatic scientist but a woman, being held in this man's embrace, with adrenaline rushing through her veins and her heart hammering against her ribs. Her body was aching to get closer, to have more. Her senses were clamoring to soak up every thrilling stimulus he telegraphed.

It gave her a heady feeling of power to know that she wasn't the only one aroused. His lips were hungry. His tongue was rapacious. His body was hard with desire for her.

For her?

He wasn't kissing *her*. He was kissing Ann.

BANTAM BOOKS BY
SANDRA BROWN

The Rana Look
Thursday's Child
Riley in the Morning
In a Class by Itself
Send No Flowers
Tidings of Great Joy
Hawk O'Toole's Hostage
Breakfast in Bed
Heaven's Price
Adam's Fall
Fanta C
A Whole New Light
22 Indigo Place
Texas! Sage
Texas! Chase
Texas! Lucky
Temperatures Rising
Long Time Coming

BANTAM

New York   Toronto   London

Sydney   Auckland

THURSDAY'S CHILD

SANDRA BROWN

This edition contains the complete text
of the original hardcover edition.
NOT ONE WORD HAS BEEN OMITTED.

THURSDAY'S CHILD
A Bantam Book

PUBLISHING HISTORY
Bantam Loveswept edition / February 1985
Bantam hardcover edition / January 2002
Bantam paperback reprint / October 2002

ISBN 0-553-57603-8

Published simultaneously in the United States and Canada

Bantam Books are published by Bantam Books, a division of Random
House, Inc. Its trademark, consisting of the words "Bantam Books"
and the portrayal of a rooster, is Registered in U.S. Patent and Trademark Office and in other countries. Marca Registrada. Bantam Books,
New York, New York.

PRINTED IN THE UNITED STATES OF AMERICA

OPM   10   9   8   7   6   5   4   3   2   1

THURSDAY'S
CHILD

Dear Reader,

You have my wholehearted thanks for the interest and enthusiasm you've shown for my Loveswept romances over the past decade. I'm enormously pleased that the enjoyment I derived from writing them was contagious. Obviously you share my fondness for love stories that always end happily and leave us with a warm inner glow.

Nothing quite equals the excitement one experiences when falling in love. In each romance, I tried to capture that excitement. The settings and characters and plots changed, but that was the recurring theme.

Something in all of us delights in lovers and their uneven pursuit of mutual fulfillment and happiness. Indeed, the pursuit is half the fun! I became deeply involved with each pair of lovers and their unique story. As though paying a visit to old friends for whom I played matchmaker, I often reread their stories myself.

I hope you enjoy this encore edition of one of my personal favorites.

—SANDRA BROWN

CHAPTER ONE

"Have you lost your mind?"

"It's a great idea."

"It's a dumb idea. We haven't done that since we were children."

"And we always got away with it."

Allison Leamon eyed her sister in exasperation. Except for the expression—Ann's was expectant—Allison could have been looking at her own reflection.

Ann was sitting Indian-fashion in the center of her sister's bed. Allison turned her back on Ann and began taking the hairpins from the bun on the back of her head. She shook out a mane of deep auburn hair that fell to her shoulders in thick waves that matched her sister's.

"Bette Davis has played twins who swapped places in a couple of her movies. Something terrible always happened."

"That's the movies; this is real life."

"Doesn't art imitate life?"

Ann sighed in vexation. "Come on, Allison. Will you or won't you?"

"I won't. I can't believe you're serious about having this operation in the first place," she said, pulling a hairbrush through her hair.

"I don't want to go through the rest of my life flat-chested."

"We're not flat-chested," Allison argued, assessing her own figure in the mirror.

"We're not overly endowed either."

"Who wants to be? They'll just sag in a few years, then you'll wish you didn't have them." Laying the brush on the vanity, she turned to Ann. "Please reconsider, Annie. Don't do this."

Ann laughed. "You're always so damned cautious and practical. Don't you ever have one frivolous thought? Just look at yourself now that you've let your hair down. You're gorgeous. Don't you want to be?"

"I'm not gorgeous. And no, I don't particularly want to be. Looks aren't important."

Ann pressed a hand over her heart and addressed the ceiling. "I know," she said theatrically, "it's what a person is like on the inside that counts."

"Make fun of me all you want, but that's the way I feel. I'd much rather be considered intelligent than a knockout."

Ann frowned in aggravation. Her sister was hopeless. All Allison cared about was her laboratory—her electron microscope, her Bunsen burner, any old organisms that could be cultivated in a petri dish! "Are you going to do me this favor or not?"

"No. I don't want any part of it. Why can't Davis know beforehand?"

"Because I want it to be a surprise."

"He likes you the way you are. Why else would he be marrying you?"

"Do you know one man who wouldn't like his woman to have large breasts?" The moment the question left her lips, Ann began shaking her head. "Forget it. I withdraw the question. You don't know any men."

"I know quite a few men," Allison said loftily.

"And they're all brainy and weird!" Ann shot back.

"They're scientists."

"As I said, brainy and weird," Ann mumbled as she plucked at a loose thread on Allison's bedspread. The sulking lasted only a few moments before she lost her patience. "I want a breast enlargement. It's for my self-esteem. Davis will go absolutely bananas when he sees the improvement. I'm asking my twin sister to help me out a little and she's making a big deal out of it."

"No pun intended, I hope," Allison said dryly. At Ann's fulminating look she relented somewhat. "You're hardly asking me to help you out 'a little.' You're asking me to pretend to be you while you sneak off and have the surgery."

"Only for a few days. Only until the bandages come off."

Allison covered her own breasts, one with each hand, and shuddered. The whole idea repelled her, but it was Ann's business. She only wished Ann hadn't involved her in it. "What about your job?"

"I'm taking a week's vacation. No problem there. You'll go to work as usual. It's only in the evenings when you'll need to be with Davis."

"What will you be doing, hiding in the back bedroom?"

"I'm staying in the clinic. It's expensive, but I'd rather stay there than at home."

Allison pushed away from the dresser and began to pace. "Annie, this is crazy. You and Davis . . . well, doesn't he expect certain, uh, you know . . ."

"You mean bedroom privileges?" Allison blushed. Ann laughed. "I've covered you on that. I told him the gynecologist changed my birth-control-pill prescription and that we weren't supposed to sleep together for three weeks until we knew they were going to take."

"That's absurd!"

"As a biologist in genetics you know that, and as a woman I know that, but *Davis* doesn't know it. He griped like hell, but he accepted it. So you won't have to worry about him trying to get you into bed. And for crying out loud, it's only for three or four days!"

Allison nervously twisted her hands. Ann had always been able to do this to her, talk her into something common sense warned against. "Switching places was an amusing game to play on Mom and Dad, even teachers, but I have a premonition that something dreadful will happen."

"You're a fatalist. Nothing's going to happen."

"And you want me to move into your condo?"

"That would be the most convenient arrangement. Davis could always find me, or rather *you,* there."

What remained unsaid, but understood, was that Allison's absence from her own apartment would go unnoticed. She had no one calling for her in the evenings. "I'd have to wear your clothes," she said unenthusiastically.

"Which will be a vast improvement over your wardrobe." Ann eyed Allison's navy dirndl skirt and tailored white blouse with undisguised distaste.

"I'll have to wear my contacts all the time and they give me a headache."

"Better a headache than those owlish glasses you wear."

"And my hair—"

"Will you stop! Your hair looks terrific loose and natural instead of knotted into that old-maid's bun." She hopped off the bed and confronted Allison with both hands on her hips. "So will you or won't you? Please, Allison. This is important to me."

Everything was important to Ann. She lived from crisis to crisis. She didn't do anything by half-measures. She plunged right into every critical event, usually dragging her unwilling, less adventuresome sister right behind her.

Allison turned to the mirror and gazed at her image. Could she pass for Ann? Ann who never met a stranger, but a potential friend? Ann who felt at home in any situation? Ann with the bubbling personality and more charm in her little finger than Allison possessed in her whole body?

Ann walked over to stand beside her. Since Allison wasn't wearing her glasses, and with her hair curling over her shoulders like Ann's, they were identical.

And it was only for a few days. And Ann was her twin, her only sibling. And lifetime habits were hard to break.

Allison smiled wryly. "Do you realize that for the rest of our lives people are going to be looking at our boobs in order to tell us apart?"

"Oh, Allison. You'll do it?" Ann spun Allison around

and gave her an exuberant hug. "I knew I could count on you. Here's my engagement ring," she said, twisting it off her finger and putting it on Allison's. "Don't dare lose it. Now let me tell you about tonight."

"Tonight?"

"Davis and 'I' are meeting his best friend for dinner. They grew up together, blood brothers and all that. I've never met him, and Davis wants to show me off."

"Oh, Annie," Allison wailed.

"Wait till you meet her, Spencer. She's terrific. Absolutely terrific. She's sweet and smart. Great figure. And her face! Heavens, her face. She's beautiful."

"She sounds it." Spencer Raft gave his friend a teasing wink.

Davis looked properly chagrined. "Am I talking about her too much?"

Spencer clapped Davis on the shoulder. "You're a man in love. You're supposed to talk about her. How long is this engagement going to last?"

Davis had met Spencer's plane at the Atlanta airport. They were negotiating the freeway traffic toward the appointed restaurant where they were to meet Ann for dinner. It was a sultry afternoon and traffic was moving with a sluggishness that matched the humidity.

"Not much longer, thank God. Last weekend of June. I want you to be my best man. Are you going to be around then or are you off again soon?"

"I'll stick around. I can't let my best friend get married without my support."

Davis glanced at the man beside him. "You know, if it

weren't for Ann, I'd envy you. Sailing all over the world in that yacht of yours, a different woman in every port, adventure, no obligations to tie you down. Must be the life." He sighed.

Spencer somberly studied the cloud-banked sunset. "It's not as glamorous as you might think," he said reflectively.

"Hell, man, share a few torrid details with your ol' buddy. I don't even know what you do."

Spencer smiled enigmatically. "It's a secret."

"You make tubs of money, work independently, work when you want to, travel all over the world. You're a mercenary, right?"

"That's classified, Davis."

Davis whistled through his teeth. "You must be linked with the CIA or something, right? No, never mind. I understand if it's classified. Just assure me of one thing."

"What's that?"

"That whatever you do is legal. No drugs or gun-running or anything like that."

Spencer laughed out loud. "I won't go to jail for what I do, no."

"That doesn't exactly put me at ease. You might be too cagey to get caught."

"I work within the law."

Davis sighed longingly. "Yep. Every once in a while I really envy you your life."

"Don't," Spencer said quietly. "I envy your happiness with Ann."

"Well, you're about to turn green with envy because there she is. Didn't I tell you she was something else?"

He braked his car in front of the restaurant just as he

spotted Ann turning the corner of the building. Jumping from the convertible, he called out her name.

She looked up, took another step, then pitched forward and fell flat on her face.

Damn!

She caught herself with her hands. The impact was jarring and caused her lower teeth to slam hard against the uppers. Her palms had been scraped and were stinging like fire. At least three layers of epidermis had been left on the sidewalk. She had tried to break her fall with one knee and the steel grate had impressed itself into her patella. She'd have a bruise for a month.

Her hair was hanging on either side of her face like a red curtain. Her rear end was sticking up in the air and she was having a hard time focusing her eyes.

And if all her physical maladies weren't enough, she had made a spectacle of herself. She could all but hear passersby speculating on which controlled substance she was high on. Davis and his friend were rushing toward her as she ignominiously tried to stand up.

Damn the high heels! She never wore them, but Ann did. The strappy sandals were lethal. But what else was she supposed to wear with the filmy chiffon dress Ann had told her to wear? Her loafers?

"Ann, darling, are you hurt?"

She came up on the foot that still wore its shoe. The heel of the other sandal was trapped in the iron grid and her unshod foot dangled lifelessly a few inches above the sidewalk.

"No, no, I'm fine," she muttered, keeping her head

down. Something was wrong, but she couldn't figure out what it was. The world didn't look right. She put her full weight down on her damaged knee. It couldn't support her yet and she felt herself falling forward again.

"Ann!" Davis cried and reached for her.

But it was another pair of arms that went around her, breaking her fall and cradling her against a chest as broad and solid as a wall. She leaned against the sturdy support for a moment, cursing her sister's influence over her and her own culpability. Why wasn't she at home with a good novel?

"Darling, you're hurt," Davis exclaimed.

"No. I'm all right. I'm just . . ."

She raised her head. This wasn't Davis. Davis had light brown hair. She got an impression of dark hair. Dark brows. A raw silk sport coat and a blue necktie. Everything was blurred. She blinked, trying to bring all the partial images together into one clear picture. She couldn't focus.

My God! I've lost a contact!

"Uh, my shoe." She wrested herself free of the strong arms and dropped to her knees once again, ostensibly groping for her shoe, but praying that by some miracle she'd locate the contact lens that must have popped out when she fell.

"Here's your purse, darling," Davis said, thrusting Ann's beaded handbag at her.

"I'll get her shoe." This voice was deep, much less rattled than Davis's. Poor Davis, Allison thought. He must be mortified by "Ann's" uncharacteristic clumsiness. What a terrific first impression his fiancée had made on his best friend.

But she couldn't worry about that now. She had to worry about getting through the evening without being able to see.

She gasped as a warm hand closed around her ankle and worked her foot into the shoe that had stuck in the grate and caused her fall.

"I'm sorry. Did I hurt you?" He touched her calf solicitously.

"No. I'm just . . ." She stuttered around something to say. *No, I'm just not used to a man helping me put on my shoe.* Brilliant, Allison. You're off to a great start. Better not to say anything.

He eased up to his full height again. It seemed to take him a long time to get there. She shook back her hair, unaccustomed to its weight on her shoulders and around her face, and much less accustomed to a man's hand on her ankle and calf. She hoped the tight grimace she felt on her mouth looked something like a smile. "I feel like such a klutz."

"Well, you looked a little klutzy," Davis said, and affectionately placed his arm around her shoulders. He kissed her temple. "Sure you're all right?"

"Of course," she said brightly, trying desperately to bring his bleary image into focus. "Is this your friend? Spencer?"

She turned toward the blurred bulk in front of her and stuck out her hand. It bumped against his sleeve. "Spencer Raft, meet Ann Leamon, my fiancée," Davis said.

"Your hand is bleeding."

"Oh, I'm sorry," she gasped. "Did I get blood on you?"

"It's all right. Here." Her hand was taken into possession by the same hard, warm fingers that had clasped her ankle. It was a strong hand. Strong, but sensitive. She felt something soft being applied with dabbing motions to her palms and when she looked down, discerned that it was a white lawn handkerchief. "I think we'd better take her home, Davis," Spencer said calmly.

"No, no," she protested. Ann would kill her if she ruined this night for Davis. "I'm fine, truly. If I could get to the ladies' room and repair the damage, I'll be fine."

And maybe Providence will provide a cane or a seeing-eye dog too, she thought.

"You're sure?" Davis asked.

"Yes, of course."

"Come on then, sweetheart." Davis, with a proprietary arm around her shoulders, led her toward the door of the restaurant. She heard Spencer following them.

As soon as they entered the elegant restaurant, she excused herself to go to the ladies' room. She hoped her limp was a good excuse for her faltering footsteps as she made her way down the dim hall. Gaining the door to the powder room, she took out her other contact and slipped on her eyeglasses. She had carried them in the evening bag.

Inspecting herself in the mirror, she saw that the damage wasn't too bad. A few whisks of the hairbrush restored her hair. She ran cool water over her palms and blotted them dry. The scrapes weren't nearly as bad as she had thought. There was a hole in her stocking the size of a quarter over the knee that had hit the grate. An inch-wide run scaled down her shin and climbed her thigh, but there was no help for that.

Thanks to the hairdo, makeup, and clothes, it was Ann who gazed back at her from the mirror. She had been dismayed when she tried on the sea green chiffon dress. Immediately she had picked up the phone and dialed the clinic where Ann had already been admitted.

"They've drawn blood and I'm due to get a chest X ray in a few minutes. Then to beddie-bye. The surgery is scheduled for early tomorrow morning."

Concerned as she was about her sister, Allison asked, "Ann, where is the brassiere you wear with this dress? Every one I've tried on shows."

"You don't wear a brassiere with that dress, silly."

"But I'm . . . it's so *bare*."

"It's supposed to be."

"I'm going to wear something else. How about the—"

"No. That is Davis's favorite dress. He requested it for tonight."

Her accident on the sidewalk had diverted her mind from the dress. Now, as she gazed at herself, she was reminded of its brevity. The shoulders were nothing more than thin straps; the scooped neck dipped low over her breasts. Why Ann would want more generous curves than they already had, she couldn't guess. She felt like she was pouring out of the dress, but there was no help for that either.

Regretfully she took off her glasses and replaced them in the purse. Then taking a deep breath, she left the restroom. Thankfully the maître d' led her to the table, otherwise she never would have spotted Davis and Spencer in the cavernous, candlelit room. They both stood as she joined them.

"Everything all right?" Davis asked worriedly as he seated her.

"Except for a run in my stocking."

"That doesn't matter. You look lovely." Davis leaned toward her and planted a soft kiss on her lips. She had to concentrate very hard not to draw back sharply.

"Thank you. I'm sorry for making such a fool of myself. I don't know what happened. I looked up when you called my name and the next thing I knew, I was picking myself up off the sidewalk."

She was sorry for Davis's sake. Davis Lundstrum had never bowled her over, but Ann adored him. He was good-looking in a clean-cut American way, generous, amiable, even tempered, and successful in his field, which had something to do with computers. She would hate to cause her future brother-in-law embarrassment.

"It was an accident," he said kindly, placing his hand on her knee beneath the table. When she flinched, he asked, "What's the matter?"

"That's my sore knee."

"Ooops, sorry, babe."

He withdrew his hand and Allison relaxed.

"I'm glad you weren't hurt," Spencer said. She turned toward him and was mildly disappointed that she couldn't clearly see his features. He had an attractive voice, stirring and deep. She knew he was tall. When he had caught her up against him, the top of her head hadn't reached his chin. He must be muscular. Hadn't she sprawled across his chest and hadn't there been room to spare?

"Davis has been looking forward to your visit."

"And I've been dying to meet you. Coming from the

airport, Davis couldn't stop talking about you," he said, laughing. "But even his lavish descriptions didn't do you justice. You're lovely and I congratulate my friend on his choice of bride."

"Th—thank you," she stammered. Rarely did she get a compliment from a man. Ann would have handled it adroitly, making some perfectly charming, flirtatious, witty comeback. Allison sat there with her knee and the palms of her hands still throbbing, with her tongue seemingly glued to the roof of her mouth merely because a man had a voice like a well-tuned cello, and with absolutely nothing to say, either charming or flirtatious or witty or otherwise.

How was she going to eat a meal without dropping half of it in her lap? When she got Ann alone . . .

And was Spencer Raft looking at her breasts? She was extremely conscious of the fact that they were naked beneath her dress and that far too much of them escaped its meager bodice. Strange, she didn't wonder if Davis was looking at her.

"Here are the drinks," Davis said. "I ordered your usual."

Allison's usual was Perrier and lime. She was afraid to learn what Ann's usual was. Her metabolism had a much greater tolerance for alcohol than Allison's did.

"Two of them?" she asked. Or, God forbid, was she seeing double?

"Happy hour," Davis explained. He raised his glass. "To old friendships. It's good to see you, Spencer."

"And you, Davis," Spencer replied, raising his glass.

Tentatively Allison reached for hers. She managed to

get hold of it and lift it to the others without making a mistake. "To good friends," she echoed. Vodka Collins, she thought, sipping the drink. Half of one and I'm under the table. Two of them and I'm unconscious. Dear heaven, how was she going to survive this? Why didn't she just blurt out the charade now before a real disaster happened? Because Ann would never speak to her again, that's why.

"Your appetizer, madam," the waiter said, waiting for her to move her arm aside so he could put the plate in front of her.

"I ordered *pâté de foie gras* for you, darling," Davis said. "I know how you love it."

She swallowed her stomach as it came lurching to the back of her throat. Pâté. No matter what fancy name they labeled it, no matter what delicacies they chopped up with it, no matter how sublimely it was seasoned, it was still liver and she'd never been able to choke down its furry texture.

"How sweet of you. But, please, the two of you must share it with me." She smiled weakly and reached to pat Davis's hand. Davis kissed her mouth softly, and it occurred to her that she had been kissed more tonight than she had in her entire life.

The waiter came to take their order for dinner. "You want prime rib medium rare, right?" Davis asked her.

She had an aversion to red meat and ate well-done beef only on an occasional cheeseburger. "I thought I might try the lobster."

Davis laughed, thinking she was joking. "Sure you did." He leaned across the table and spoke to Spencer confidentially. "The last time she ate shellfish she broke out in hives. It was ghastly, but spreading on the calamine lotion turned out to be great fun."

"I'll bet it did," the deep voice hummed.

"By the time we finished, I had more on me than she did on her."

Both men laughed. Allison blushed to the roots of her hair as Davis kissed her ear and growled. "Darling, if you want to play that game again, just ask. I won't put you through another allergic reaction first."

She closed her menu and pretended to laugh. "That was horrible, wasn't it?" Why hadn't she remembered that Ann was allergic to shellfish and why was the idea of playing bedroom games with Davis totally beyond her comprehension?

When their order had been given, Davis excused himself to go to the men's room. The waiter offered to remove the appetizer plate, and Allison jumped at the chance to get rid of it. She'd managed to eat three crackers with the foul stuff spread on them and had washed each one down with a long swallow of her drink. The alcohol was making her head buzz and her ears ring.

Uncomfortably aware of the man sitting with her, she fumbled for her cocktail glass, found the stirrer and twirled it idly. Spencer Raft leaned closer. He wore an elusive cologne that made her want to go in search of its source.

"That was a hard fall you took. Are you certain you're all right?" he asked softly.

His breath drifted over the side of her neck and down her bare arm. "Of course. I'm fine." His face was definitely masculine, with hard planes and sharp angles, but she still couldn't make out the features distinctly. That frustrated her for reasons she couldn't define.

"You're drinking out of both glasses," he whispered, and though she couldn't see his smile, she could hear it in his voice.

"Am I?" she gasped, then tried to emulate Ann's delightful giggle. "How silly of me."

"And you didn't eat all your pâté when Davis expounded on how much you love it."

Ann had told her this old friend of Davis's was some sort of mercenary involved in intriguing business deals that took him all over the world. Whatever he was, he was no fool and much more perceptive than Davis.

"I'm nervous."

"Why?"

"Because of you."

"Me?"

"Davis wanted you to be impressed with me."

What a glib thing for her to say. Maybe she wasn't a lost cause for small talk after all. That would please him, flatter him, make him laugh lightly and settle back in his chair like any man who had just had his ego stroked.

To her alarm, rather than moving away, he leaned closer.

"Then relax. I'm impressed."

Again, she couldn't see his expression, but she could *feel* it. It was there, riding on his tone of voice—suggestive, insinuating, sexy. And she was the one being stroked. She could feel his eyes raking down her chest, over her breasts, homing in on their crests, which seemed to respond like slaves to his compelling voice.

She was grateful that Davis returned at that moment. Her heart was hammering and nervous moisture was now lubricating her abraded palms. Despite her sore knee, she crossed her legs and held them tightly together.

"Tell me about the wedding," Spencer said, as though they'd been chatting about the weather.

This was safe territory. She knew the plans for the wedding because Ann discussed each minute detail with her. "It's a church wedding, but it will be small and not too formal. I'm having only one attendant, my sister. And, of course, you'll be Davis's best man."

"You have a sister?" he inquired politely.

"Yes." Davis chuckled as he sipped his Scotch.

"What's funny?" Allison demanded.

"I was just thinking about Allison."

"What about her?"

"Oh, come on, honey. You know I'm not putting her down, but you've got to admit she is strange."

"Strange?" Spencer asked.

Before Allison could respond, Davis took it upon himself to expound. "They're twins. To look at them you can't tell them apart, but in every other way, they're as different as daylight and dark."

"We're different, yes, but what do you mean by calling Allison strange?" She had been trying her best to make this evening a success for Davis and now he was insulting her; unwittingly, yes, but it hurt just the same.

"Well, the way she acts, the way she dresses." He turned to Spencer. "If there's ever been a candidate for spinsterhood, she's it. The only sex she cares about is in her laboratory. She got all excited the other day because two rare bugs had mated."

"It was *mice*. Her work is extremely important," Allison flared.

"I'm not saying it's not, but—"

"What kind of work?" Spencer interrupted.

"Genetic research," Allison retorted sharply, defensively, almost daring the man beside her to make a derisive or lewd comment about it.

But Davis supplied that. "Who cares about the sex lives of cockroaches?" he asked. "She handles all these creepy, crawly little creatures. Yuk!" He made a face and shuddered.

"We should all care about the work that I . . . that Allison does. It's important to our quality of life for generations to come. And she's never done anything on the sex life of cockroaches!" she finished heatedly.

Diplomatically, Spencer said, "The research sounds fascinating."

Davis smiled at Allison apologetically. "I'm sorry, hon, maybe I was teasing too hard. Spencer might enjoy meeting Allison. He's a whiz kid too."

Allison took another sip of the vodka Collins and wondered if the drink or her self-defensive outburst was responsible for making her feel better. "Oh?"

"Yeah, he's a real brain. Phi Beta Kappa. Rhodes scholar."

Allison looked at Spencer with new interest. She had expected him to be the kind of man she instantly despised, the kind who viewed women as sex objects and considered nothing more important than their physical satiation. Apparently he had some depth even though he was an irresponsible adventurer.

"I'd like to meet your sister—Allison?—sometime," he said. "Who does she do research for?"

"Mitchell-Burns."

"Ahh," he said, nodding. He was apparently familiar with the company that manufactured pharmaceuticals and chemicals, and sponsored research in every field from medicine to energy conservation.

The waiter served their dinner. Allison forced herself to eat the blood red meat and to sip the blood red wine, while she had no liking for either. Beverages served at room temperature were fine if you lived at the North Pole. Otherwise, she preferred ice in everything that wasn't scalding hot.

The wine, combined with the vodka, wasn't doing her impaired vision any good either. She was groping for a tumbler of water when her hand collided with her wineglass and knocked it over. It landed on Spencer's sleeve and spread a ruby stain over the raw silk.

"Oh, my," she said, splaying a hand over her bare chest. "I'm sorry."

She never cried. Ann had always been the one prone to burst into tears at the drop of a hat. Now Allison had an overwhelming need to weep. She must be terribly drunk, or terribly embarrassed, or terribly hurt.

And why shouldn't she feel hurt? Tonight she'd learned what a humorous topic of conversation she had provided for her sister and Davis. How many other people thought of her as an eccentric old spinster, vicariously living out her sex life through her laboratory animals? The thought disgusted her and her stomach threatened to rebel against the food it was being forced to digest.

"Oh, it's spreading." Ineffectually she blotted at the stain with her napkin.

"Forget it."

"Darling, are you sure you're all right?" Davis asked. "You haven't been yourself all evening."

Then, just as much as she had wanted to cry, she wanted to laugh. "I'm fine," she struggled to say around the hysterical laughter bubbling in her throat. "I guess I'm still shaky after my fall." Feeling another wave of remorse, she looked toward Spencer. "I'm truly sorry about your jacket."

"Make it up to me."

"How?"

"Dance with me."

She sobered instantly. "Dance?" she squeaked.

CHAPTER TWO

"Go on, Ann," Davis said. "That'll make you feel better. You love to dance."

True. Ann did love to dance and she did it with grace and natural rhythm. Allison had never mastered the art. Their mother had insisted on both of them taking ballet and ballroom dancing. Even Allison's best efforts had been disappointing.

"Please," Spencer Raft said, standing and extending his hand. "Unless your knee still hurts."

"Oh no, my knee is fine." *It's my two left feet I'm worried about.*

What choice did she have? She had collapsed into the man's arms before they'd said their first hello. She had bled on his handkerchief. She had ruined his sport coat that cost three hundred dollars at least. If he was willing to dance wearing a wine-stained sleeve, she should be willing to with a run in her stocking. If she refused,

Davis would no doubt get angry with "Ann" for being ungracious to his friend. Allison couldn't let that happen.

She laid her napkin aside and stood. His hand folded around her elbow and turned her away. "We'll be right back, darling," she said to Davis over her shoulder.

With a flash of panic, she felt that they were deserting him forever. The man who steered her toward the small dance floor seemed to have an uncanny ability to get people to do his bidding. She imagined that he had no trouble leading a woman anywhere, even from beneath the nose of her hovering fiancé.

If it were really Ann being pulled into his arms and pressed against a body that defined masculinity in its rawest form, she would have been concerned for her sister's future with Davis.

But it wasn't Ann.

It was Allison who obeyed the subtle commands of his hands and arms and moved without hesitation into his embrace. She had consumed much more than her quota of alcohol. The evening had been just as disastrous as she had predicted it would be. She was weary of pretending to be somebody she wasn't.

So, for all those reasons, she let herself be molded against his protective warmth. As a little girl wanting to hide, she would pull a blanket over her head, thinking that no one could see her if she couldn't see them. She felt that way now. The world looked unfocused and diffuse and she was hiding behind that cloudy vision. Later she couldn't be held accountable for the outcome.

But wasn't it odd that she could effortlessly follow Spencer Raft's dance steps when she'd never been able to follow another man's lead? Even in the high heels, she moved in time to the music, swaying against his body with perfect rhythm.

"Despite what you say, you don't feel well, do you?" His lips moved in her hair. His breath was fragrant and warm against her cheek.

"I'm dizzy," she admitted. More than that, each internal organ had gone weightless and was looking for a new place to settle.

He cupped the back of her head and pressed it onto his chest. Then his fingers sank into her hair and began to massage her scalp. Her eyes drifted shut, but immediately sprang wide. What was she doing? "Please, Spencer," she said, resisting his hand on the back of her head and trying to lift it. "I . . . Davis—"

"Shhh, it's all right. You've had a rough night."

He had maneuvered them to the far side of the dance floor. Other couples were between them and the table where Ann's trusting fiancé sat waiting. The lighting was dim. He probably couldn't see Spencer's hand strumming up and down her back anyway.

"You shouldn't hold me this way," she protested feebly, letting her head obey the dictates of his hand. She laid it back on his chest. The hard curve of his breast seemed sculpted to fit into the hollow of her cheek.

"No, I shouldn't. I'm not proud of myself for doing it either," he murmured. "Davis is my best friend." His arms tightened a fraction. "But you feel so good against me. I knew you would."

It did feel good, this perfect meshing of two opposites. She didn't remember a time when she had been more consciously aware of her body. Always before, her mind had ruled her. Now her body was demanding that she take notice of it.

Her skin felt feverish, but the heat emanated from the inside out. Had her breasts ever felt full and heavy as they did now? Why were her nipples drawn and straining against the flimsy bodice of Ann's dress? And why did she want to rub them against his chest? Her limbs felt too leaden to move, but her heart was pounding energetically. She felt each pulse beat in the center of her womanhood, which was warm and restless and swollen with an unnamed ailment.

Nor had she ever been so aware of another human body. All her senses were attuned to him. She was considered tall, but he dwarfed her. He was rock solid from the shoulder on which her hand rested to his thighs that moved against hers. Even without her hands confirming it, she knew his arms and legs were bunched with sinewy muscles.

But he wasn't all brawn. His physical strength didn't override his sensitivity. He was capable of tenderness. Even now his thumb was pressing slow circles into her palm and the fingers of his right hand were sifting over her bare shoulder. "I've never seen a redhead with skin like yours. Don't most redheads have fair complexions?"

"We, my sister and I, inherited our complexions from our maternal grandmother. She was Spanish and had olive skin. We got our green eyes from her too."

"And the red hair?" He combed through it, dragging his fingers through the heavy tresses with a sensuous lack of haste.

"Our Irish grandfather."

"A very colorful family."

She laughed against his shirtfront. "In more ways than one."

"Your twin for instance?"

She lifted her head then to look up at him. "Davis led you to believe she's a freak. She's not."

He touched her cheek. "Is she as pretty as you?"

"Thank you." Disconcerting as it was to be held close, she found it more disturbing to peer up into his face, hear that hypnotizing voice, and still not be able to discern exactly what he looked like. She let her forehead fall forward into the hollow below his shoulder. "We're identical. But very different."

"How so?"

"She wouldn't let you hold her this way." That's it. Blame this irresponsibility on Ann. No, on Allison. That's who they were talking about, wasn't it? Oh Lord, it was becoming too confusing to muddle through. She couldn't think. What mental powers were left her were slipping in proportion to how close Spencer held her.

"I'd better go back," she said, squirming free.

"No. They've started another song." His arms didn't release her. Short of causing a scene that would humiliate her, anger Davis, and threaten a lifetime friendship, she let him pull her against him once again. "How long have you and Davis been engaged?"

"Almost a year."

"Do you love him?"

"Of course!" she exclaimed.

"Do you?" Spencer persisted.

She lowered her eyes. Compared to her lying, her dancing was like Ginger Rogers's. Since she was old enough to talk, she'd never been able to lie her way out of anything. "I love him very much," she said stiffly.

"Do you live together?"

"No." Davis had asked Ann to move in with him several times, but in deference to their parents, she had refused.

"But you sleep together."

Her cheeks flamed with embarrassment and anger as she glared up at him. "That's none of your business."

"I want to know," he said stubbornly.

Just as stubbornly, she said, "Certainly we sleep together."

"Is your sex life satisfactory?"

"Wonderful."

"Liar."

Flabbergasted by his audacity, her feet stopped dancing. "How dare you say such a thing to me."

"How dare I? I'll tell you how I dare. If your sex life with Davis were as 'wonderful' as you say, your body wouldn't be so hungry." He hauled her close again, pulling them together so tightly that the breath left her lungs on a soft whoosh. "And it *is* hungry, Ann." He made a thrusting movement against her hips and, before she could stop it, a telling moan departed her lips.

Angry with him and ashamed of herself, she pushed away from him. She bumped into only two couples as she made her way across the dance floor and back toward the table. Davis stood and took her hand. "Feel better now?"

"Much." Her knees buckled just as she found her chair. She was trembling all over and hated herself for it.

She was behaving like a schoolgirl in the arms of a man to whom seduction was an idle pasttime. He could probably speak fluent eroticism in sixteen languages. Ann, madly in love with Davis, wouldn't have allowed herself to be held like that, spoken to in that bold a manner. She would have laughed it off, or slapped his face, or kneed him in the groin, or *anything* but curl up against him like a homeless kitten who had just been taken in on a stormy night.

If she succumbed to Spencer Raft's charm at all, Davis would be furious, not with Allison but with Ann. Ann would never speak to her again if she jeopardized her relationship with Davis. And she—

Well, she was certainly not going to be swept into a tidal wave of passion by any man. She knew better. That kind of romanticism wasn't for a practical thinker like her.

She had had a lapse of common sense for the length of one dance. So? No harm was done. Any animal, when stroked and petted, purred with contentment. It wouldn't happen again. She would avoid the man like the plague.

For the rest of the evening she devoted all her attention to Davis and responded to Spencer's conversation only to satisfy etiquette. She had seen Ann with Davis and imitated her sister's demonstrations of loving affection. Davis was convinced. He basked in her evident fondness for him. Allison didn't risk looking at Spencer to gauge his reaction.

Once outside, Davis had the doorman hail a taxi for Spencer. "Here's the address of my apartment and a spare key." He handed his guest a slip of paper and a key. "I want to follow Ann home and see that she gets there safely."

"I don't blame you," Spencer said. He stepped forward,

lightly laid his hands on her shoulders and dropped a friendly kiss on her cheek. "Good night, Ann. You're everything Davis said . . . and more."

His hands fell away as he stepped back, but the imprint of them burned on her skin. This man with the captivating voice and large, hard body posed a threat she couldn't begin to understand. She looped her arm through Davis's as though clinging to him for protection. "Thank you, Spencer. Good night. It was nice to meet you at last."

Only when the cab pulled away with Spencer Raft inside did she begin to breathe normally.

It was tricky, but she managed to sneak her eyeglasses on and drive home without Davis detecting that she was wearing them. She whipped them off as she swung Ann's car into the driveway and turned off the ignition. The glasses were safely in her purse by the time Davis joined her at the front door.

She unlocked it and he followed her inside with a familiarity that alarmed Allison and presented her with another sticky situation to get out of.

"Good night, darling," she said.

" 'Good night, darling'? I feel like saying hello. I haven't kissed you properly all evening."

Before she could avoid it, he pulled her into his arms and planted his mouth over hers. Her initial reaction was to clamp her lips shut, but she knew that would never do. So she allowed him to kiss her thoroughly. Her hands rested tentatively on his waist.

"Oh, God, Annie," he whispered against her ear when he finally released her lips. "I've missed having some privacy tonight. What did you think of Spencer?"

She couldn't think of anything while her sister's fiancé's hand was sliding down from her shoulder and over her breast. "Uh . . . he was ch—charming, just as you said."

"That's what he said about you. I had told him how gorgeous and sexy you were. He agreed wholeheartedly."

"Oh!" The exclamation burst out involuntarily when he slid the strap of her dress down and pushed it aside.

He jumped back in surprise. "What's the matter?"

"N—nothing. I just, uh, I made such a fool of myself in front of your friend. I was afraid you'd be mad."

He took her in his arms again and hugged her tight. "I'll admit I was dismayed to see you do a pratfall on the sidewalk." He laughed. "That would have been more like Allison." Then from arms' length he ran his eyes up and down. "You're not still hurting anywhere, are you?"

"No." Allison the klutz, Allison the spinster, Allison the diverting topic of conversation flashed him a quick, insincere smile with rubbery lips. "I'm fine."

"Good," he growled. His lips moved down her neck as his hand fondled her breast, lifting it out of her bodice.

She panicked and pushed away. "Davis!"

"What?" He put his hands on his hips and faced her with that belligerence unique to a sexually thwarted male. "What's the matter with you tonight?"

Allison wanted to tell him in no uncertain terms that nothing was the matter with her, that it was her prerogative to say no if she damn well felt like it. But Ann wouldn't do that. What would Ann do if she didn't feel like sex but wanted to turn him down easily?

She raised a fluttering hand to her throat. "Nothing's wrong. I just—" Desperately she groped for a logical explanation. Ann had said he wouldn't expect her to go to bed with him because . . . Why? Oh yes, the pills. She forced her face into one of Ann's softly feminine smiles. "I just don't want to get something started that we can't finish." For good measure, she ran her hand up the placket of his shirt and brushed her fingers back and forth over his chin.

"Yeah, I guess you're right." He ran an exasperated hand through his hair. "How much longer?"

"Not much." Her eyes were misty with promise. "I can't do without much longer." She'd heard that line in a recent movie, but did lovers really talk this way?

"Neither can I, baby." He drew her to him and kissed her chastely. Well, almost chastely. "I'd better leave now."

"All right." She looped her arm around his waist and walked with him to the door. "Good night." She came up on her toes and kissed his lips.

"Good night." He ran a caressing hand over her fanny. She smiled at him woodenly and waved good-bye until he was in his car and on his way.

As soon as she shut the door, she braced her back against it, closing her eyes and inhaling long, deep breaths. She had survived it. Except for falling down on a public sidewalk and letting Davis's playboy friend dance too close, nothing too calamitous had happened. How many more nights to go? Two? Three? Maybe she could pretend to have one of those messy stomach viruses tomorrow night.

With that encouraging possibility in mind, she went into Ann's bedroom. She had packed a few of her own things to bring with her, among them an old shirt of her father's that she usually slept in. It had been pilfered

from his closet years ago. She slept with the long sleeves
rolled back. The tails struck her at mid-thigh.

She cleaned her face and brushed her teeth. Remembering that she had a spare contact in her overnight bag,
she put it in to try it. What a wonderful world it was
when one could see! She sighed her relief that at least she
wouldn't have to call the ophthalmologist and get another lens.

Just as she was about to take out the contacts and get
into bed, the doorbell rang. Davis? Had he forgotten
something? She slipped through the shadowed rooms on
bare feet, the hem of the shirt whispering against her
thighs. Opening the door, she peered around it, keeping
her body hidden.

"Hello, Ann."

She made an odd sound that was half gasp, half sucking breath. He was beautiful. All the blurred edges and
unfocused features came together in stark clarity and she
was awestruck at the handsome combination of ruggedness
and polished charm.

Dark hair, attractively out of control. A broad, intelligent forehead underlined by eyebrows that were rogu-
ishly shaggy, yet expressive. Eyes that pierced through
her like blue lasers, so deep was their color, surrounded
by spiky black lashes.

His nose was the envy of any ever stamped on a coin.
His mouth . . . Her stomach sank to the floor of her body
at her first clear sight of the sensuously fashioned lips,
the lower just a tad sulkier than the upper.

Every feminine cell in her body responded to the
sheer maleness it now confronted. Her breasts began to

ache; the nipples tingled. Soft tongues of arousal were licking the insides of her thighs. She felt butter-soft and malleable from the tip of her head to the tips of her toes that were now curling into the deep pile of her sister's carpet. She, who had never placed much importance on one's physical appearance, was reacting solely to Spencer Raft's good looks.

She only hoped all the chaos going on inside her wasn't obvious. She inched farther behind the door. "Davis is already gone."

"I know. I saw him leave."

"What are you doing here then?"

"I came to see you."

Not her. Not Allison. He had come to see Ann. "Well, you shouldn't have."

"I know that too. But I'm here."

"How did you get here?"

"I rented a car and looked up your address in the phone book. Then I left a message for Davis, telling him not to expect me until later. Are you going to invite me in?"

"No."

"Then I'll have to come in on my own." With hardly any effort, he pushed the door open and stepped inside.

She was left standing with nothing to shield her except the oversized shirt that was sheer and soft after years of frequent washings. Unless he was as blind as she without her glasses, he would know that she wore nothing under it but a skimpy pair of bikini panties and a becoming rosy blush.

The blue eyes took their time touring her, stopping

frequently at places that deepened the warm color spreading over her. His eyes seemed to burn right through the cotton and touch her skin, kiss it, brand it.

He studied every feature of her face for a long time. "You've got incredible hair." He reached for a wavy strand that was lying beguilingly across her shoulder.

"And you've got incredible nerve." She swatted his hand away and took a step back. She was angry and had to admit that in part her anger was due to the fact that he thought she was Ann. Had she come to the restaurant tonight not with cascading red hair and slinky chiffon, but as dowdy ol' Allison, he would have been polite, but he wouldn't be here now stripping her of her dad's shirt with hot, knowledgeable eyes.

"Because of Davis, you mean?"

"Of course because of Davis," she cried. "I doubt he knows his best friend is paying a late-night visit to his fiancée."

"You're right, he doesn't."

"He thinks the world of you. All I've heard since I met him is Spencer this and Spencer that. Now——"

"All right," he snapped, effectively interrupting her. For several tense moments he studied the floor between his Bally loafers. When he lifted his head again, there was anguish in the blue eyes and an expression of regret on his mouth.

"Do you think I planned on being attracted to you? Do you think I planned on this happening?"

"Nothing is happening."

She felt a frantic need to protest, not only for Ann's sake but for her own. Because something *was* happening. And it was the first time it had happened to her. Before

meeting Spencer Raft she had thought the idea of imme-
diate, combustible sexual attraction was the bait used by
advertisers to sell perfume and toothpaste. Not so. It was
real. "Nothing's happening," she repeated to convince
herself.

One of his brows arched in query. "No?"

She switched her weight from one bare foot to the
other and wet her lips nervously. "No."

"You're lying again, Ann. If you weren't experiencing something you feel guilty about, you would have
welcomed me with a friendly smile and invited me in,
probably suggesting that we locate Davis and have a midnight snack together."

He was right. That's what Ann would have done. But
she wasn't Ann! Why not just tell him? Why not just
laugh and say, "Look, you're not going to believe this,"
and then tell him about Ann's scheme?

Because then she'd have to cope with him. And if she
couldn't handle him while pretending to be Ann, how
could she hope to handle him as herself?

He sensed her consternation and his expression soft-
ened appreciably. "You're thinking the worst of me. May
I tell you about myself so you won't think this is something I do often?"

"You don't meet and seduce women often?" she asked
frostily, daring him to deny it.

He grinned and her haughtiness thawed. Nothing female could withstand the sexy heat of that smile. "I don't
meet and seduce my best friend's girl, no. Even for someone as jaded and worldly as I, this is a first."

His teasing piqued her. "Davis has told me how you
sail around the world in that boat of yours. He says that

you're an adventurer, a mercenary of some sort. I'm sure you're playing this game to amuse yourself, but I don't think it's funny. Now please leave before I—"

He took a step nearer. "Before you what?"

She swallowed and backed up even as he advanced. "Before I have to call Davis and tell him what you're up to," she said breathlessly.

"And what's that?"

"Seducing me." Her back met with the wall and there was no more room to retreat. He kept coming toward her until his long legs straddled hers and his hands were braced against the wall on either side of her head.

"Is that what I'm doing?" His breath fanned her face. He exuded a blatant sexuality that lapped against her like incessant waves.

"Aren't you?"

A smile tugged at the corner of his mouth. "That's for you to say, isn't it? I can only confess that I'm trying my damnedest to seduce you. You're the only one who can say if it's working."

Oh, it was working. She was melting against the wall and her head was getting foggy. Her pulse was finding new places to throb—shameful, forbidden, marvelous places.

"When we were dancing, you felt it, didn't you?" He ducked his head and nuzzled the side of her neck with his nose.

Her eyes slid closed. Yes, she had felt it. She hadn't studied biology for ten years without knowing about all the operative male parts. And his parts operated beautifully. She had felt him, rigid and thick, when he thrust his hips against her softness. How could she help but feel such ready desire, such evidence of arousal, such unabashed manliness?

But she had some pride left. "Felt what?" she asked huskily as she pried her eyes open.

"That tickling sensation that starts somewhere around here." He pressed the tip of his index finger into her tummy. "And feathers its way up and around here." That same finger zigzagged its way up the valley between her ribs to her breasts and indolently circled one. "Until you feel it in the back of your throat." He gently probed that shallow triangle at her throat's base. "Before it floats, floats, floats, to land with a soft explosion somewhere about"——his finger slid down her middle, past her navel, to stop at her bikini line; he opened his hand and pressed his palm over her——"here." He finished on the merest of whispers.

She groaned and her head fell forward onto his chest. "Don't, please." The repercussions of that soft explosion undulated through her like the widening ripples in a pond that had been undisturbed for years.

He cradled her face between his hands and raised it. "I hate the thought of betraying my best friend. The last thing I would ever want to do is hurt Davis. So you must know what an impact you made on me if I'd risk destroying a lifetime friendship to come to you like this."

"You shouldn't have."

"If I had listened to my conscience I wouldn't have."

"But you didn't listen."

"I couldn't hear it over the pounding of my heart."

"This is impossible."

"Is it? Let's find out."

Her lips first felt the pads of his thumbs. Alternately

they glided over her lower lip. Then his breath, moist and warm, misted over them. When he first touched her lips with his, an arrow of pleasure shot through her from the point of contact to the heart of her femininity, where it punctured open pockets of feeling she didn't know were there.

The sensation was so new, so soul-shattering, that, in alarm, she cried his name. "Spencer."

"Oh, yes," he whispered before wrapping his arms around her and eliminating the space between them.

One arm went to the small of her back, the other across her shoulders. He pulled her against him possessively. His head tilted to one side and his lips slanted over hers. He pressed harder, investigating the seam of her lips with his tongue.

At its damp, velvety touch, her lips parted. That was all the invitation he needed. His tongue sampled the sweetness of her mouth. It prowled hungrily, restlessly, aimlessly, until he was certain she acknowledged his right to be there. Then he thrust it in and out with an evocative rhythm as his body moved against hers.

Poor Ann, Allison thought. She would go through life settling for Davis's bland kisses without experiencing this. It was like comparing a soft rain to a tempest. Davis's kiss had been pleasant and refreshing, but it had no thunder, no wildness, no delicious savagery, no exciting ferocity. Davis's kiss had been mildly stimulating. Spencer's was unapologetically wanton. Davis's kiss involved only his mouth. Spencer's employed his whole body.

He lifted her shirt, slid his hand past her waist to her derrière and, with a sustained pressure she was powerless to resist, brought her high and hard against him. He tucked himself cozily into the V of her thighs and a growl of pleasure rumbled through his chest and into hers.

His other hand found her breast beneath the cotton shirt and kneaded it lovingly. His thumb gently massaged the tip. When it peaked hard he murmured her name. His lips sipped at hers. "Ann, Ann. I knew it would be like this with us."

Her sister's name was like a slap in the face that jerked her out of a trance. She freed her lips from his and twisted away from his caress. Surprised, he released her and she stepped from between him and the wall. Standing in the middle of Ann's living room, eyes squeezed shut against her uncharacteristic behavior, she clasped her hands tightly at her waist, trying to regain her equilibrium.

When she finally turned to face him, he was watching her closely. She knew he was keeping his distance, not because he wanted to, but in order to give her time to sort through her thoughts.

"You must leave, Spencer. Now. And forget that . . . that kiss ever happened."

"If you ask me to, I'll leave, but I won't forget that kiss."

"You must!" she cried anxiously.

He thought she was Ann. Tonight she had been Ann, but tomorrow she would go back to being frumpy, brainy Allison again and he wouldn't give her a second look. But besides all that, this *thing* that was going on between them could ruin Ann's relationship with Davis.

"I can't forget it," he said firmly. "I didn't intend to walk into that restaurant and immediately start wanting my friend's fiancée, but I did. When I left, I thought maybe

I had been fanciful. Maybe it had been a trick of the candle-light that made you the most desirable woman I'd ever met. Or maybe I had just been jealous of how Davis felt about you."

He took a step nearer, but when he reached out to touch her, she shrank away. His face took on a stern and determined expression. "But now I've kissed you. And it took the top of my head off. Do you really think I'm go-ing to turn away, go on my merry way, and forget it hap-pened? No way. I'm not made like that."

"You go after what you want, is that it?"

"Yes."

"And damn the consequences."

His mouth tightened in an effort to curb his temper. "Despite what it looks like, I'm a man of honor. I want you, Ann. And by every indication I think you want me. But there's Davis to consider. I'll have to do something about that, won't I?"

With that oblique statement, icy cold panic shot through her. She clutched at the collar of her shirt with white-knuckled fingers. "What do you mean, you'll have to do something about that?"

"Leave everything to me." He took three striding steps toward her and kissed her soundly.

"No, Spencer, listen. You mustn't—"

He kissed her again. Then, while she was trying to regain her breath and reset the world on its axis, he let himself out.

Allison stared at the closed door for ponderous sec-onds. Covering her mouth with a trembling hand, she said, "My God. What have I done?"

CHAPTER THREE

At one o'clock the following afternoon Allison stopped at the nurse's station in the clinic to inquire about Ann.

"She's still in the recovery room, but you can go in."

The nurse gave her directions and Allison made her way down the tiled hallways. They were unlike ordinary hospital corridors. These halls witnessed no tragedies but were decorated with fine lithographs, illuminated by track lighting, and lined with lush tropical plants. Rather than sympathize with the patients occupying these rooms, one could almost envy them the serene, restful surroundings.

After having spent a sleepless night, Allison had telephoned the clinic at seven A.M. only to be told that Ms. Leamon was already on her way to surgery, that she would be anesthetized for several hours, and to check back around noon.

There were two other patients in the post-op room. Both were being attended by nurses. Ann was in the bed nearest the door. Her eyes were closed, but the I.V. and other surgical paraphernalia had been removed. She lay sleeping with her arms at her sides. Beneath the hospital gown Allison could detect the bandages. She grimaced.

"Annie?" she whispered, taking her sister's hand and squeezing it. "Annie?"

Ann's eyes struggled open and blinked Allison into focus. "Hi." She seemed to roll the word around in her mouth like a marble before it finally came out.

"How are you?"

"Fine. Very sleepy." She winced as she moved her shoulders. "I'd feel really lousy if I didn't know how sensational I'm going to look in my bikini from now on."

Allison tried to smile, but it came across as a worried frown. Despite her grogginess Ann chuckled softly. "Don't look so worried. I'm fine, really. The doctor said"—her speech slurred and her eyelids coasted down before she forced them to open again—"said everything was perfect."

"Good. I'm glad. When will they take you to your room?"

Ann's head slumped to one side on the stiff pillow. "Soon, I guess," she said thickly. Her eyes closed again.

Allison felt helpless and awkward. She had gotten little sleep last night worrying about the dilemma Ann was in at her making. All morning she had fretted about what she was going to do to set things right. The first thing was to tell Ann everything that had happened. But Ann was in no condition to listen.

"Annie?" she ventured, shaking her twin's hand. When the green eyes ventured open again she said, "Let me call Davis. He would be frantic if he knew you were going through any kind of surgery without him. He should be here holding your hand, not me. He'll be very upset with you when he finds out you kept this a secret from him."

"Please, Allison, no," Ann croaked from a dry throat. "Not yet."

"But he should know."

"He will. I don't want him to see me until the bandages come off and I'm beautiful."

"How you look doesn't matter. He loves you."

"Please, Allison, do this for me." She closed her eyes again and gave every impression of having fallen asleep. Allison wondered if she was playing opossum. As a child Ann had avoided many hassles by pretending to be asleep.

"I'll call you later," Allison said dutifully, releasing Ann's listless hand and leaving the room.

She couldn't help but be aggravated with Ann. Ann had dumped this mess in her lap, now she was sleeping through it. Meanwhile Allison was floundering for a solution. "Well, it won't be my fault if her engagement falls apart," Allison vowed as she pushed through the heavy door of the clinic into the bright Georgia summer sunlight.

But she knew it would be her fault. Everyone would blame her for the fiasco, including herself.

All the way back to the lab, she tried to absolve herself of guilt, but none of her arguments was convincing. She had danced with the man. She had let him into Ann's house. She had allowed him liberties she would have ordinarily quelled with one killing look. She had permitted his kiss.

And she had kissed him back.

An overbearing playboy was making a play for Ann, whom he had actually never even met. He was going to wreck a perfectly wonderful relationship by making it a triangle when none of the three involved was really privy to what was happening. She, an outsider, was responsible for the whole mess and yet powerless to do anything about it at the risk of making herself look like a desperate spinster who had impersonated her sister in order to win a man's kiss.

The dilemmas Bette Davis had gotten herself into were nothing compared to this doozy.

Of course, I might be borrowing trouble, she thought as she entered the building that housed her laboratory. She might never see Spencer Raft again. He was the type who would steal a kiss from his best friend's fiancée for his own perverse satisfaction and then go on to greener pastures. Davis had said he never stayed in one place long. Perhaps even now he was on his way back to Hilton Head, where his yacht was docked, ready to sail away to new horizons.

Allison frowned, remembering his determined expression as he'd let himself out last night. He didn't look like a man who could be swept away by the winds of fortune. He didn't look like a man who would trust his future to whimsy. He looked like a man who directed his own fate. And if he would steal kisses from a woman forbidden to him, what else would he try to steal?

The thought made her so nervous that she could barely concentrate on the experiment she'd been working on for months. It was an important experiment on the influence of heredity and environment on intelligence.

Allison had always been fascinated by the conflicting theories on what determined intelligence. She was convinced there was a "middle road" between those who believed I.Q. was genetically based—the nature school—and those who were sure that the environment played the more important role—the nurture school. Today, though, this usually spellbinding subject and her experiment with it failed to distract her from thoughts of Spencer. She could only manage to focus enough during the afternoon to chronicle her experimental results in the lab journal.

"Smart little booger."

It was late. The sun cast long, slanting shadows on the floor. At hearing her supervisor's voice, Allison glanced over her shoulder. Dr. Hyden peered at a rat that was separated from some others in a divided cage.

"Isn't he, though," she said proudly. "That's Alexander the Great."

"Born smart," the scientist commented. "Like you." Dr. Hyden tweaked the tip of her nose affectionately.

Ever since taking the job at Mitchell-Burns, she had worked with Dr. Dirk Hyden, whom she adored. He had an appealing mustiness about him and epitomized the absent-minded genius. He often searched for eyeglasses perched on top of his balding head; there was usually a smorgasbord of food stains on his necktie; his lab coat was always clean, but rarely ironed. But he was a leader in their field, and she had been fortunate to be assigned to his team. Their admiration and affection was mutual.

Allison peered at Alexander the Great, poking her finger into the cage to rub him gently. There was a thoughtful expression on her face.

"You don't seem very excited that your experiments are proving your hypotheses to be correct," Dr. Hyden remarked.

"Oh, I am. It's just that I have something else on my mind. My sister had surgery today."

Dr. Hyden's bright eyes clouded. "Nothing serious, I hope."

"No, no, nothing serious," Allison reassured him. "I'm just concerned about her."

Dr. Hyden could appreciate her dedication to their program, but he wished she had something outside the lab to round out her life. Such singlemindedness in a young woman wasn't healthy. Through their years of working together, he had come to think of her in fonder terms than as just another gifted scientist. "What will you start on next?"

"More work on the correlation between intelligence and nutrition."

"I'll look forward to reading your proposal with all the specifics," he said, catching his lapels with his hands and rocking back on his heels. "It's a pity we can't match human beings for breeding, isn't it?"

She laughed. "It would be a scientist's dream to take a perfectly matched couple, physically and mentally, mate them, document the fetus's growth. Then once the child was born, nurture his body and his mind on a carefully planned regime. Who knows, by the time he started first grade, he might be ready to read Shakespeare."

Dr. Hyden cocked his head to one side. "You'd be a good mother for such an experiment. Got any potential fathers in mind?"

She laughed and, shrugging off her lab coat, went

to hang it up. "Disregarding the father, I hardly think I qualify."

"Why not? You're highly intelligent, a perfect physical specimen of the species, and I know a few young men around here who would agree with me."

"The men around here respect me as a scientist. They hardly lust after me as a sex object."

"Do you give them a chance?"

She closed the door on the metal locker and turned toward him. "How's *your* sex life, doctor?"

He blushed to the roots of his sparse, grizzled hair. "I'm sorry. I was meddling." He came to her and placed his hands on her shoulders. "You work very hard. You should play more. Go out tonight. Drink some wine. Dance."

She laughed, mirthlessly this time. Last night she had gone out, drunk wine, danced, and gotten herself entangled in an impossible mess. "I'm not much of a party girl. But thanks for caring." She patted his cheek and left.

The telephone was ringing when she let herself into Ann's condo. "Hello?"

"Ann, hi, darling."

It was Davis. "Hello."

"Where have you been all day?"

The automatic response of "At work" died in her throat. Ann was on vacation. She had told Davis she would be running wedding-related errands. "I've been shopping."

"Buy anything?"

Would he want to see her purchases? "A few surprises

for you. Postwedding surprises." Did she sound like Ann, like a coy, simpering bride-to-be?

"Yum-yum. I can't wait." His voice went from a lecherous whisper to brisk efficiency in one breath. "I have a surprise for you too. Spencer and I will pick you up in about fifteen minutes."

"Surprise?" The last thing she needed was another surprise. Spencer had been enough of one. "Spencer's coming along?"

"Yes. I invited him. You don't mind, do you?"

"No, of course not. I'll enjoy seeing him again." No doubt that's what Ann would have said. But then Ann would never have let last night happen. Nor would Ann's palms be filmed with nervous perspiration at the mention of the man's name and the thought of seeing him again.

She glanced down at her khaki skirt, the equally dull blouse, and the low-heeled brown shoes she had worn to work. "Is this a dress-up or casual surprise?"

"Definitely casual," Davis said. "Spencer and I are going to play racquetball afterward."

"All right. I'll be ready. Fifteen minutes?"

"Right, sweet." He blew a kiss into the telephone before he hung up.

The image her mirror reflected back wasn't too encouraging. She'd have to hurry if she was to bring about a transformation in only fifteen minutes. She shed her clothes and inspected the contents of Ann's closet, which were as colorful as hers were drab. Despite their vivid coloring, Ann wore every shade in the rainbow and somehow managed to bring about stunning results.

Allison selected a pair of linen slacks that Ann had

called melon, but that Allison called orange, and a matching cotton knit pullover.

She slipped on sandals that had brightly colored beads threaded on the thongs to decorate her bare toes. Taking the pins from her hair, she brushed it to fall lustrously against her shoulders. She made a pass along her eyelashes with a black mascara wand, whisked blusher across her cheekbones, and glossed her lips with peachy color. She was misting on the fragrance Ann preferred when the doorbell rang.

"Hiya," Davis said the moment she pulled open the door. Snarling affectionately, he put his hands on either side of her waist and pulled her to him. His mouth came down on hers with a fervor that robbed Allison of breath. It was all she could do not to pull away from his embrace. But for the benefit of the man standing behind Davis, she locked her hands around his neck and poured her heart and soul into the kiss, praying that God and her sister would understand.

Ann hadn't specified what she should do about open-mouthed kisses. What else could she do but kiss back as Ann would? Davis's kisses certainly didn't arouse her. Not like . . . But she couldn't think about that.

When he finally raised his head, she laughed softly and rubbed her fingertips across his lips to pick up the traces of lip gloss she'd left there.

He drew her close again and nuzzled her ear. "I missed you today." His hands caressed up and down her back. "Why did you wear a bra?"

As an intelligent person, she had pledged that she would capably handle any situation that should arise tonight. Yet now, not thirty seconds into the evening, she floundered for an answer to his whispered, intimate inquiry.

She pressed her lips against his ear. "Because you were having such a hard time last night resisting temptation. And you know that we can't—"

"I gotcha," he murmured against her cheek. "But I don't like it." After another swift kiss, he stepped aside so she could greet Spencer.

"Hello, Ann."

It felt as if his voice reached inside her, plucked a heartstring, and its private message was being thrummed throughout her body.

"Hello, Spencer," she said with counterfeit gaiety.

Her knees went to jelly as their gazes locked. His eyes were like steady blue flames beneath the untidy shelf of eyebrows. His face was well acquainted with salt air, sea, and sun, but each squint line had been artistically etched to add to his appeal rather than to detract from it. His limbs were lean and tan and hard with muscle. He had on white shorts and a blue knit shirt that was stretched over the contours of his torso. Chic European sunglasses had been pushed to the top of his head and nestled in the tousled dark hair.

For protection against his appeal and to support her quaking body, she linked her arm through Davis's. "Has Davis kept you busy today?"

"He took me through the computer plant," Spencer said amiably. "It's quite an operation."

"Yes. It fascinates me too." She squeezed Davis's arm and made certain Spencer saw the prideful gesture.

"Davis told me you work with computers too. What do you do?"

Her smile collapsed. Why hadn't she listened more carefully when Ann prattled on about her job? "I . . . uh . . ."

"She's too modest to tell you that she's the programmer for the whole company."

Allison blessed Davis with a genuine loving smile. He had rescued her. "Well, I'm on vacation this week and don't want to talk about my job. What is my surprise?"

Davis grinned conspiratorially at Spencer. "Shall we keep her in suspense a while longer?"

"Don't you dare!" Allison exclaimed just as Ann would have and playfully gouged her fist into Davis's stomach. His wasn't nearly as flat and taut as Spencer's, which looked like a pickax couldn't make a dent in it.

"I found a house today that I want you to see. I think it's just what we've been looking for."

"Oh, darling, how wonderful." She flung her arms around his neck. Ann and Davis had been house shopping for months. Allison knew that Ann's reaction to this news would be overabundant enthusiasm. "Where is it? Is it affordable? What's it like?"

Davis laughed at her with delight. "Come on and we'll show you."

She rode in the front seat with Davis but was constantly aware of Spencer sitting behind them like a brooding bodyguard. She kept her hand resting on Davis's knee.

Comparisons between the two men were irrelevant, but she couldn't help making them. Davis's legs hadn't been exposed to as much sun as Spencer's. They looked pale and spongy. Allison was loath to touch him, but her fingers itched to brush over the springy hair dusting Spencer's copper-colored skin and to test the steeliness of the muscles.

However, these thoughts were subliminal. She concentrated on showering attention and affection on Davis and congratulated herself on doing quite well.

Her spirits sank when Davis braked his car in front of the house he was so eager to show off. Ann would have loved it. Allison hated it.

It was single-storied, low, and streamlined. There was no steep slope to its roof, no gable windows under sheltering eaves. It was brand spanking new, but lacking in character.

"Oh, Davis," she said, hoping she didn't sound as despairing as she felt.

Even the yard looked artificial. Each shrub was uniform and lined up with the precision of a military regiment. Still, Allison gushed over the landscaping as Davis led her up the sidewalk to shake the hand of the toothsome realtor in the polyester suit who unlocked the front door for them.

The interior smelled of paint and wallpaper paste, not aged wood paneling and freshly baked bread. Most of the rooms were perfectly square, having no interesting niches in which to tuck a bookcase or an antique English tea table. The fireplace in the living room looked too sterile ever to build a fire in. It didn't invite one to curl up in front of it with an oversized pillow and a spy novel. The kitchen was more clinical than Allison's lab. She couldn't imagine these immaculate countertops being dusted with flour, or anything spicy and delicious bubbling over on the pristine range.

"Wait till you see the master bathroom," Davis enthused, dragging her down the narrow white hallways that reminded her of a mental hospital.

The bathroom had a sunken marble tub and built-in basins. She had always wanted a bathtub with claw feet and a pedestal sink with brass faucets.

"You're not saying much," Davis said apprehensively.

Allison whirled around to face him and placed a reassuring hand on his arm. "I'm overwhelmed." Much as she detested the house, she knew Ann would love it. On numerous occasions she had described what she wanted, and this house fit that description to a T. "I don't know what to say. It's . . . it's . . ."

"I don't want to influence your decision. You really like it?" he asked, anxiously peering into her eyes.

"Of course. I love it. You knew I would." She hugged him so he couldn't look into her eyes. He might detect her contacts, or worse, the lie she was telling him.

"Mr. Lundstrum, I'd like to show you the worktable in the garage," the realtor said.

Davis cuffed her under the chin and excitedly followed the realtor out. She was left alone in the master bathroom with Spencer. Since entering the house, he had trailed them from room to room, but had failed to make a comment other than when asked a direct question.

"You don't like it, do you?"

She spun around, irritated and dismayed that he could read her so well. "I love it. You heard me tell Davis that I did."

"Yes." He closed the distance between them. "That's what I heard you tell Davis, but you're lying."

"I am not!"

"I knew this house wasn't for you. You'd like something warm and cozy with shuttered windows, at least one of them with stained glass in it. A staircase with newel posts. Unusual rooms with character. Floorboards that creak."

"It sounds like a haunted house."

Another step brought him even nearer, until she had to tilt her head back to look into his face. "You haunted me last night. I couldn't sleep. Did you?"

"Like a baby."

He raised his hand and traced the violet shadow beneath her eye with the tip of his index finger. "No, you didn't. You lay in your bed and thought about our kiss just as I did. And when you got up this morning it was still on your mind. It has been all day. Hasn't it?"

"No," she whispered. There was an edge of desperation in her voice that even she could hear.

"You've been thinking about how instantaneous the attraction between us was."

"No. I didn't think about—"

"And the way our mouths meld together."

"Don't talk—"

"And the way your breast fits my hand. The way we fit perfectly all over."

"Stop! If Davis should overhear—"

"Why are you doing this, Ann?"

"What?"

"Pretending to love Davis."

"I'm not pretending. I *do* love him."

"Perhaps, but not enough to marry him."

"I'm going to marry him."

"Out of duty? Why? Do you feel guilty because he fell harder for you than you did for him? Why are you committing yourself to an unhappy marriage? That's not doing Davis any favor either. Sooner or later he'll realize how you feel."

"I won't listen to any more of this." She made to move past him, but he circled her upper arm with strong, tapering fingers.

"I know what you think of me and I know why. Davis has mistakenly glamorized my life. He's painted me to be a rich playboy, vagariously yachting around the world, sleeping with a different woman every night."

"Don't you?"

He smiled that bone-melting grin. "Hardly. I work very diligently at what I do."

"Which is?"

"Which is beside the point. I'll admit that when I first bought the boat and started traveling, it was great fun. Adventure in different countries, with different cultures, with different women."

"Spare me the lurid details."

"I intend to. My point is that I've grown up. I'm tired of living only for myself. I've been searching for something. But not until last night when I held you in my arms did I know what it was."

"Don't say—"

"Listen to me," he commanded, shaking her slightly. "I didn't count on this thunderbolt either. I know you're as shocked by it as I am. I hate like hell that you belong to Davis. He's my best friend. We've loved each other like brothers. But I'll be damned before I let three people become miserably unhappy."

An image of Ann's face swam before her eyes. Her expression was accusing. Was she going to stand here listening to tantalizing words and ruin her sister's life? She struggled against the romantic web he was spinning around her. "I'm not unhappy. I love Davis."

"You go through the motions of loving him," he said softly, almost sympathetically, as though he understood the tremendous sacrifice she was making. "You kiss him and touch him. But I can sense your restraint." He grasped her shoulders then and pressed her against him. "There was no restraint in the way your body conformed to mine last night, was there? And you know as well as I do that when I kissed you it wasn't just a kiss, it was making love."

To prove it, he repeated it.

His mouth came down on hers with tender possession. He whispered love words against her lips, making promises that his tongue fulfilled as it dipped into the receptive warmth of her mouth. It probed deep, went in search of her tongue, and stroked her toward a desire that finally engulfed her. She slumped against him and encircled him with her arms.

Allison Leamon had never thought she wanted this kind of romance. There wasn't room in her life for it. It was superficial and fleeting and only fools believed in its authenticity.

Didn't she know better than anyone that sex was mechanical? It was purely biological and physical and had little or nothing to do with the emotions. Any two creatures of the same species could mate. It required nothing of them but properly working reproductive organs.

But here she was, no longer a pragmatic scientist but a woman, being held in this man's embrace, with adrenaline rushing through her veins and her heart hammering against her ribs. Her body was aching to get closer, to have more. Her senses were clamoring to soak up every thrilling stimulus he telegraphed.

It gave her a heady feeling of power to know that she wasn't the only one aroused. His lips were hungry. His tongue was rapacious. His body was hard with desire for her.

For her?

He wasn't kissing *her*. He was kissing Ann. Should this Ann in his arms, by some Cinderella-like spell, revert back into Allison, his desire would immediately evaporate. He was kissing a redhead who had the panache to wear orange pants and barefoot sandals with flirtatious beads on the toes. Who could drink two cocktails without getting tipsy. Who liked sophisticated foods like pâté de foie gras and houses with precultivated lawns.

And who, most assuredly, had the good sense not to let her fiancé's best friend kiss her with provocative intimacy.

She pushed him away. Her breasts were heaving, her lips were red and dewy from his kiss, her eyes tearbright. "We can't do this anymore, Spencer."

"I know." He stepped away from her and glanced over his shoulder as he heard Davis and the realtor returning. "As long as you have that," he indicated the diamond ring on her left hand, "I can't touch you again. It goes against every principle I believe in to go on betraying my friend. Davis will have to be told how I feel. I'll take care of it somehow."

Wildly she gripped his rock-hard biceps. "You'll take care of *nothing*. You'll tell Davis *nothing*. Do you hear me?" she whispered frantically as she heard Davis approaching. "I'm marrying Davis Lundstrum and that's all there is to it."

She saw the resolution hardening his jaw and knew she was getting nowhere. Ann's future was hovering on the brink of disaster and it was her fault. Despite the humiliation it would bring her, she had no choice but to tell him the truth. "Listen, Spencer, there's something I have to tell you. I'm not—"

"Hey, you two, you ought to see that garage," Davis said as he came in. "We can park both cars in there, honey, with room to spare."

She had lost her chance. The charade must go on.

Allison rushed into Davis's arms. "I love the house, darling. But not nearly as much as I love you."

As soon as she got safely inside Ann's condo, she went to the telephone. Davis and Spencer were going to play racquetball, then have dinner with several of Davis's friends. "You don't mind me taking a night out with the boys, do you?"

"Of course not, darling." If only he knew how profound her relief was. But she pouted in a way she had seen Ann do and laid a hand on his chest. "As long as it's not too often."

He gave her a thorough kiss that could have been a

handshake for all the impact it had on her. The good-byes seemed to take an eternity. Allison couldn't wait to close the front door behind him.

After the second ring, Ann picked up the telephone in her room. Her voice still sounded cottony from the anesthetic.

"Annie, I've got to talk to you and I want you to listen."

"Hello, Allison."

Instantly contrite for her seeming lack of concern, she asked, "How are you feeling?"

"Only a little uncomfortable because of the bandages. The anesthetic has made my stomach queasy."

"I'm sorry, but—"

"How are you? How's work?"

"Work?" *Work?* She didn't want to talk about work when she felt like a mountain was about to cave in on her. "Work is fine. Annie—"

"What did you do today?"

Allison sighed and rubbed her temple where a demon was tapping it with a hammer. "I'm working on heredity in relation to intelligence."

Ann's laugh was garbled. "You should have a baby. Think what a little genius he'd be."

Now the demon was banging both temples. "Yeah, that's what Dr. Hyden said. The problem is finding an equally brainy father. Listen, Ann, I didn't call you to talk about my work. We've got a real problem. Davis took me to see a house today. He loves it and I think you will. But how can we be sure? I can't make a decision like this for you."

"Calm down, Allison. I'll go see the house as soon as I leave the clinic."

"You don't understand the urgency. The realtor pressed Davis to sign a contract. I demurred, saying I wanted to think about it. I told Davis I was stalling in hopes they'd lower the price, but . . . Annie, are you listening? Are you still awake?"

"Yes," she answered groggily. "What's the house like?"

Allison described it. "I think it's just what you want."

"I trust your opinion. Go ahead and agree to the contract."

"No. Not on your life. If you hate the house, you'd be stuck with it and I'd be responsible."

"All right, then," Ann said tiredly. "Keep stalling them."

"I can't!" Allison cried.

Davis could be stalled. Spencer couldn't. In the few hours she'd known him, one aspect of his personality had become eminently clear. Once he made up his mind about something, hell or high water wouldn't stop him from acting on it. He might do something dreadful before the truth came out.

"I'm bringing Davis to the hospital in the morning," Allison said.

Davis and Ann would be reconciled. Spencer would see how madly in love they were. He would go away or stay and fight for her. But in any event, Allison would be out of it.

"Oh, no, please don't," Ann said, showing a burst of energy. "Allison, you promised."

"It's making me crazy pretending to be you. Put yourself in my place. Would you want to pretend to be me, even for a little while?"

Ann's lengthy silence was her giveaway. "No, I

wouldn't. But I don't want Davis to know yet. Just another day or two. Please."

Allison gnashed her teeth with frustration. Taking another tack, she lowered her voice to a confidential pitch. "Annie, you know how affectionate Davis is. He kisses me all the time. Just the way he kisses you." She let that sink in, then added, "Do you know what I'm saying?"

"I know what you're trying to do, and it won't work. I'm not jealous of you, Allison. I know what you think of men and, much as you love Davis like a brother-in-law, don't pretend that you're getting shamefully aroused by his kisses. It would take more than a few kisses to get your motor started."

Wanna bet? If only Ann could see her in Spencer's embrace, she wouldn't recognize her spinsterish sister with the cold motor. It didn't even require a kiss. One look from him and she was off like a rocket.

"I haven't hurt your feelings, have I?" Ann asked.

"No."

"You know how attractive I think you are. All I meant was that you can't blackmail me into letting you tell Davis about my operation." She laughed softly. "Kiss him all you want. The practice will do you good."

Ignoring the last comment, Allison sighed in resignation. She had tried. She had tried to tell Spencer but had been interrupted. She had tried to convince Ann but had failed.

"All right, Ann. I'll continue being you for another day, but there might be consequences. I hope you're prepared to face them."

"There won't be any consequences. Once Davis finds

out, we'll all have a good laugh and he'll be delighted
with what I've done."

Yes, but what about Spencer? She didn't want to bring
his name into it. It would be better if Ann never knew
how she'd felt about Davis's best friend.

"Good night. Rest well. I'll try to come by at lunch
tomorrow."

"Good night, Allison. And thanks. I know this can't
be easy for you."

That was the understatement of the century.

She was bent over a microscope studying a slide. Her
eyes had been so tired from another sleepless night that
her contacts had felt like hot pokers. She had finally taken
them out and put on her glasses. Her hair was pulled into
the efficient knot on the back of her head. She was wearing an olive green dress under her lab coat. Unfortunately her shoes were as ugly as they were comfortable.
She wore no jewelry in the lab, but there was a pencil
propped behind her ear.

This ensemble was a far cry from the orange slacks
and tarty sandals.

"Ms. Leamon? Allison Leamon?"

Her head popped up and she turned around abruptly
at the piercingly familiar sound of his voice. She froze as
he stepped into her world, invading it, altering it, filling
it, and shrinking it.

"Yes?" she said hoarsely.

"My name is Spencer Raft."

CHAPTER FOUR

Reflexively she took a step backward. The small of her back came up against the marble-slab table and there it stayed, as though secured by a magnet. She was rendered motionless and speechless by disbelief.

Wearing an open, friendly smile, he advanced into the room. When he was but a few feet from her, he subjected her to a thorough appraisal.

"It's incredible," he whispered. "You really are identical." Finally he shook his head slightly, widened his grin and said, "Forgive me for staring so rudely. As I said, my name is Spencer Raft."

No doubt he expected her to extend her hand to be shaken, but she couldn't move. Much less touch him. Much less touch him with hands that still bore faint scratches on the palms. And after the kisses they had shared, wasn't a handshake a little ridiculous?

"Allison Leamon." Halfway through her name, her

voice vaulted from the low register to the high like an adolescent boy's.

"I've recently come to know your sister. The likeness is remarkable. Except for the eyeglasses you're exactly like her."

She couldn't continue standing there like a statue. She would have to talk to him. "Ann mentioned your name. You're Davis's friend, aren't you?"

"Yes." He studied her face for a moment longer, before taking in the lab. Perfectly at ease, he wandered toward the animal cages that housed rats and mice, a family of rhesus monkeys, and several generations of rabbits. "Ann told me about your work. It sounds fascinating."

Was he being condescendingly polite or did he really think so? "I believe it is."

He turned, puzzled by her stilted, almost hostile, tone. "I'm not interrupting you at a critical moment, am I?"

"No." Ashamed of her rudeness, she forced herself away from the false security of the table. "I was only doing some preliminary work for an experiment I'm going to start on soon."

She moistened her lips and tried to relax. It wasn't easy. He was the last person she would have expected to come through the doors of the lab. Now that he was here, her feelings about his sudden appearance were ambiguous.

On the one hand she was afraid he would detect the deception. On the other hand, she was vaguely disappointed that he hadn't come in, looked at her closely, and recognized her instantly.

In a melodramatic scenario her mind played out, she could see him rushing toward her and saying, "My darling, do you think I wouldn't know you anywhere?" He would pull the pins from her hair and it would cascade over his plundering hands. He would bend her back over his arm and sear her lips with his. His anxious hands would tear open the buttons of her dress and he would bury his lips in the valley between her breasts, declaring his love and passion in fervent murmurs.

What a fool I am! she thought to herself. She would never allow a man that kind of undisciplined access to her.

"What will your next experiment be about?" Spencer asked.

Now he was simply asking her a polite question; he was hardly in the throes of passion. And certainly no recognition had dawned in his eyes.

She pushed her eyeglasses higher up the bridge of her nose. "I'm going to measure the difference a balanced diet can make in one's intelligence."

"Can it?"

"Can what what?"

"Can a balanced diet make a difference in one's intelligence?"

"Other experiments have proven that. I'm testing to what degree it makes a difference."

"I see. Go on."

This was the first conversation they'd ever had that wasn't directly related to themselves. If he was merely being mannerly, he was a good actor, because he appeared to be genuinely interested.

She crossed to where he was standing near the cages

and briefly explained the protocols for her initial work with mice. She glanced up to see if he'd lost interest yet. He hadn't. His eyes were riveted on her.

"And then what?" he asked.

"And then I'll do the same with the primates."

She poked her finger into the monkey cage. The youngest sailed across it and caught her finger playfully. "This is Oscar. He's terribly spoiled." Reaching into her pocket, she took out a peanut and gave it to the baby monkey. He began nibbling on it greedily.

At the sound of Spencer's husky laughter, her stomach did a somersault and she glanced up at him again. "Your work sounds exciting," he said.

"Sometimes it can be. Mostly it's routine, redundant, and requires a tremendous amount of patience. Nature doesn't always work quickly." And then again it can smite you right between the eyes in the course of a few minutes.

Oscar had eaten his peanut and was now tugging on Spencer's finger, which he had stuck through the bars of the cage. "Are the lab animals expensive?"

"Yes. But since we're not doing disease research, ours have a longer life expectancy. We breed them for experimentation. So that actually serves a dual purpose."

"You're a matchmaker."

At his teasing inflection, she braved another look up at him. God really should have broken the mold once Spencer was created. He would never exceed this specimen of man. "Usually the mating is done clinically."

"Artificial insemination?"

"Yes."

He cast a quick glance at Oscar's parents and gave the

male monkey a sympathetic smile. "That hardly seems fair." When he looked down at Allison, his eyes were alight with mischief.

She swallowed hard and avoided his eyes as she asked, "Would you like some coffee, Mr. Raft?"

Without waiting for his answer, she turned toward the far side of the room where a table held a coffeemaker and a selection of chipped mugs, along with a variety of sweeteners and a powdered creamer.

"Thank you, yes. Black," he said, following her. "And please call me Spencer." Without invitation he sat on a tall stool and hooked the heel of his shoe on the second rung. The position pulled the fabric of his casual gray slacks tight over his thighs. And his lap.

Again Allison found it necessary to swallow hard. Her hands were trembling so badly she could barely pour their coffee. In a desperate effort to cover her nervousness, she said, "I'm always glad to show someone the lab, but I don't think that's why you singled me out for a visit."

She passed him a cup of coffee and when he took it, their eyes met and held for a lengthy second. "You're right, Allison. I came here to talk about Ann."

Taking up her own coffee mug, she leaned against another high table. "Ann? What about her?"

"I want to go to bed with her."

Allison showered her lab coat and the front of his hundred-dollar Perry Ellis sport shirt with hot coffee. The coughing and sputtering went on for what seemed like hours while her eyes streamed and she tried to keep from strangling.

Spencer had one hand on her shoulder while the other solicitously thumped her back. "There. Better?" he asked when several seconds had passed without her coughing.

"Yes, better," she wheezed.

"How about a drink of water?"

"Please."

He carried an empty cup to one of the deep basins, filled it with tap water, and returned it to her. She sipped tentatively at first, still not certain if all the pipes were reopened. When she had drunk all the water, she dabbed at her eyes with the hem of her lab coat. Spencer passed her a handkerchief, the second one he'd given her in forty-eight hours, but he didn't know that.

"Thank you," she said, handing it back to him. "I'm sorry I stained your shirt."

He assessed the damp spots, which were already drying. "It will wash. Are you sure you're all right?"

"Yes. It's just . . . What you said . . . you—"

"I should apologize. I didn't intend to be so blunt. I presumed that since you were twins, you and Ann confided in each other."

"Oh, we're very close. I just didn't expect you to come right out and say . . . what you said."

He grinned engagingly. "Frankness is one of my faults, I'm afraid. I don't waste time beating around the bush."

"Yes, I know," she mumbled.

"Pardon?" he said, leaning forward on the stool.

She recoiled quickly. "Nothing. I just said that you're in for a disappointment. Ann is marrying Davis in a few weeks. She's terribly in love with him."

"Is she?"

"Yes."

"You know that for a fact?"

She knew that for a fact. Ann loved Davis. "Yes. He's all she talks about." She tried for a confident smile. It came across as sickly. She could *feel* how sickly that smile was.

He vacated the stool with one lithe movement and began to pace. Turning his back on her, he crammed his hands into the pockets of his slacks. This time they stretched over his seat. Allison's eyes dropped to the lean tautness of his hips. Was she becoming obsessed? Possessed? She didn't remember ever looking at a man's buttocks before. What was it with her lately? If it wasn't his face making her stomach float light as a feather, it was the front of his trousers, or, now, the back of them.

"I disagree with you, Allison," he said, turning abruptly. Her eyes sprang back up to his face. "I don't think Ann loves Davis as she professes to."

"Wh—why do you say that?"

"Because I've kissed her and I don't think any woman who loves a man enough to marry him would respond to another man's kisses the way she does to mine."

"Oh, you've kissed her," she said in a small voice.

"Please understand that I've never been one to kiss and tell. I never discuss my sex life with 'the guys' or anyone else. This is one exception." He ran a hand through his hair. "Ann is an exception."

She had taken her glasses off when she began to choke. Now she slipped them back on to hide the confusion in her eyes. She knew she was as easy to read as a banner headline and he was as smart as a whip. "Exception? How is she an exception?"

He lifted those jewellike eyes to hers and she thought

her knees would give way. "I don't know how to express it. I want her in a way I've never wanted another woman. It's not just lust. I could slake that with any woman. It's . . . hell, I don't know. I feel like an idiot standing here talking to you like this. You know what a captivating creature your sister is."

Captivating? Her? Did he know who she was after all? Was he making fun of her? "Ann told me about meeting you. She said she made a fool of herself."

He laughed softly and sat down on the stool again. His tension had ebbed. His bones and muscles were now loose as he slouched forward slightly. Long legs stretched out in front of him and he clasped his hands between his thighs.

"Yeah, it was a rather inauspicious beginning."

Allison picked up a paper napkin, ostensibly to blot at the coffee stains on her lab coat. Actually it was to give her an air of nonchalance. "If she behaved as clumsily and awkwardly as she described, how could you, a man who's urbane and attractive and sophisticated, a man who squires women from all over the world, how could you be attracted to m . . . uh, Ann?"

He cocked one dark eyebrow and peered up at her through a forest of black lashes. One corner of his lips curved into a lazy grin. "Who said I was urbane and attractive and sophisticated? Ann? Did she talk to you about me?"

"Some," she said evasively, tossing down the napkin. It was becoming a shredded, damp wad of paper in her sweaty hand.

"I guess it would be ungallant to ask you what she said," he probed hopefully.

"I can't repeat what my sister told me in confidence."

His head went back and he sighed. "Ah, well, I have to respect that. But in answer to your question, I was attracted to Ann first because I think she's beautiful." He smiled fondly. "She was so valiant after taking that undignified fall, which would have humiliated most women to tears. I've never seen a woman show such staunch character. She wanted so badly for the evening to go well for Davis's sake. I could tell that pleasing him and making a good impression on me were very important to her. Unselfishly she pulled herself together and put up a good front for the rest of the evening. A woman with that kind of moxie, I just had to get to know better."

She wanted to bask in his compliments to her character but couldn't afford to. He was smitten by Ann's looks, not Allison's. She grasped one point he had made and used it to convince him of Ann's devotion to Davis.

"You said she was determined to make the evening a success for Davis's sake. Surely that indicates how much she loves him."

He stood, frustration making his shoulders hunch as he slid his hands into his pockets once again. Damn! She wished he'd stop doing that. "She plays at being in love with him. And I think she does love him, fondly, as a friend."

"She loves him in every way," Allison declared.

He faced her belligerently. "Then why does she shrink away from his embraces?"

"She doesn't."

"She does. Watch them the next time you're around them. It's a momentary, unconscious thing. Her body doesn't gravitate toward his the way a lover's usually does, it retreats. Is that normal? No. I think she feels duty-bound to him. He ordered her dinner, but she didn't like it. She only pretended to for his sake. She pretended to love a house he'd picked out, but she didn't."

Allison jumped in. "Ann loved the house. She told me so."

"Then she was lying to you and to herself. If you'd been there, you would have seen what I'm talking about."

Allison twisted her hands as she gnawed her lower lip. This was her chance to convince him that Ann was wildly in love with her fiancé, yet he was shooting down every argument. Because he'd been observing her for the last few days instead of Ann, she didn't have much ammunition. All his observations were right on target.

"She lets him order her food to boost his ego, you know, to make him feel important and essential to her."

He gazed at her, his jaw slack with incredulity. "To boost his ego? You mean like some outdated sexist role-playing? The dominant male and the submissive female who never makes a decision on her own?"

She shifted her shoulders nervously. "Something like that."

He smacked his forehead with the heel of his hand. "I don't believe it! Ann's smarter than that. You mean she'd consign herself to living in a house she didn't really like just to keep from hurting his feelings, to keep from bruising his ego?"

"It's their business, not mine, or yours."

"I've made it mine," he said, almost in a shout. "I don't believe in that kind of hypocrisy, do you?"

Her eyes met his steadfastly. His demanded the truth

and she answered him, not as Ann would, but as she, Allison, felt. "No, I don't."

"I don't think Ann does either. Not really. She's only gotten herself into a rut she doesn't know how to get out of."

"Maybe she likes that rut. Did you ever stop to consider that?"

"Maybe she did until a few days ago."

"Until she met you?" Allison challenged.

"All right, yes. As conceited as it sounds, I think she's beginning to see that she doesn't have to have a chauvinistic relationship with a man."

"You don't think it's chauvinistic to say you want to get her into bed?" Allison demanded angrily.

He had the good grace to laugh self-deprecatingly. "Guilty as charged. But," he held up his hand, palm out, "she wants to make love with me just as much as I want to with her."

Allison's irritation vanished under an onslaught of embarrassment. She went hot all over. "Why do you say that?"

"By the way she's responded each time I've held her. I don't have to explain to you, a biologist, the physical symptoms of arousal. As a man, I recognize them in a woman."

She tried to clear her throat of the congestion lodged there. "No, you don't have to explain anything to me." She picked up her coffee mug and swirled the contents as she stared into it. "If Ann should break her engagement to Davis and . . . come to you, what did you have in mind?"

"In mind?"

It was the hardest thing she'd ever done, but she lifted her eyes to his. They flickered away quickly, lest he see that her curiosity was anything but idle. "After . . . after . . ."

"After we've become lovers?" Her eyes flew back to his. He was teasing again. But after enjoying her blush that so reminded him of Ann's, he grew serious. The bushy brows V'ed with perplexity. "I honestly don't know, Allison. I would never make a woman promises I didn't intend to keep, but I don't think this is a passing fancy that would be over quickly. She intrigues me. I think it would take me a long time to discover everything about her that I want to know." He sighed and raised his hands to his sides, letting them fall again. "That's as honest as I can be."

"I appreciate your honesty," she said gruffly, staring down at her toes. "As Ann's sister," she rushed to add. For the past several moments she had almost forgotten that they were speaking of Ann, not her. Getting back on track she said, "Surely, if you feel anything for Ann at all, you won't ask her to sacrifice the security of marriage and a home for an indefinite affair with you."

"I would never hurt her."

"You would! If she jilted Davis for you, she could be terribly hurt later on."

"How?"

"By you sailing away in your yacht and leaving her without anything, that's how."

"But she wouldn't be trapped in an unhappy marriage with a man she didn't love."

"She loves Davis. You said so yourself." She paused

to draw a deep breath. "May I offer an opinion?" He conceded with a nod. "You're different from any man Ann has ever met. Perhaps you've swept her off her feet. She's temporarily dazzled." She wet her lips with a quick flick of her tongue. "But I swear to you she would never sacrifice her happiness with Davis for a casual affair with you."

He took hold of her hands, thankfully touching only her fingers. "You're a sensible young woman, Allison."

Sensible. Yes. She wore sensible clothes and sensible shoes and a sensible hairdo. She could converse sensibly about any number of subjects. She had a level head on her shoulders. But without the feminine trappings of her identical sister, she was only that. Sensible.

But there was nothing sensible about the sizzling currents racing up and down her arms at the touch of his hands. Her eyes lacked all traces of sensibleness as they drowned in the deep blue of his. With his softly hoarse, compelling voice he could have commanded her to go to the edge of the world and jump off, and she would have complied.

But he was seeing sensible Allison. He didn't recognize her as the woman who stirred passion in him. She was amazed how much that hurt her.

"Tell me the truth," he went on. "After all I've told you, do you think what I feel for Ann is 'casual'? Do you think I'd gamble away my friendship with Davis for a casual affair? Apparently you have a jaundiced opinion of me. I'll admit I've had my share of women, but I'm made of better stuff than to wreck a beautiful love affair between two people for my own selfish gratification and then go blithely on my way."

His thumbs were rubbing the backs of her fingers. He charmed even when he didn't work at it, and Allison hated herself for being susceptible.

"Do you honestly think Ann is head over heels in love with Davis?" he asked softly.

"Yes," she said sincerely. "I know she is."

Sighing, he stepped back and released her hands. For a long moment he stared out the tall, wide windows onto the manicured lawn of the complex.

"I'm sorry, Allison. I know you're probably closer to Ann than anyone on earth. But I disagree with you. I guess you'd have to be a man. You would have had to hold her and kiss her to understand what I'm talking about. I rely on my instincts. They've never failed me. They're right this time too."

He smiled down at her. "Good-bye. I'm sure we'll meet again. And I'd rather you not mention this visit to Ann."

He turned to go, but she stumbled after him. "What are you going to do?"

At the door he paused. "I don't know. But I hate subterfuge. I believe in laying my cards on the table in every relationship, business or personal." At her anguished expression, he flashed her a confidence-inspiring smile. "Don't worry, Allison. Everything will work out for the best."

He left her. She was still twisting her hands and her bruised lower lip was still caught between her teeth.

Spencer was dejected as he left the Mitchell-Burns plant and retraced his steps to where he had parked his rented car. Such a sentiment was foreign to him and he didn't know how to handle it.

He got in the car, rolled down the window, and leaned his head back to think.

Now what? He had sought out Ann's twin in the hope of having her provide him with some insight, some inkling of hope. Rather, Allison seemed convinced that Ann was in love with Davis.

He was disappointed. He was angry. And he was frantic.

That slipping self-confidence irked him most of all. Women had always been an easy commodity. If he saw one he wanted, he took her. If there were complications not worth the effort or risk, he figuratively doffed his hat and went away without a wistful backward glance. No great loss.

This was different. If he didn't have Ann, he would feel the loss for a long time. He knew that just as instinctively as he knew that, despite Allison's claims to the contrary, Ann wanted him too.

This fluctuation between wanting her and feeling guilty about it was going to drive him crazy. If she loved Davis, what choice did he have but to give her up to him? Davis had seen her and loved her first. On the other hand, if she was as attracted to him as he was to her, they were already hurting Davis. Spencer had always been an advocate of fair play. Why couldn't the three of them be honest with one another, meet the problem head on, discuss it like mature adults?

After he had given himself that fighting chance, he would accept the outcome.

Getting out of his car, he walked to the pay telephone

booth at the front of the building. He consulted the Yellow Pages, then dialed the number.

"Mr. Lundstrum, please. . . . Spencer Raft. . . . Yes, I'll hold." As he waited, he tapped his finger against the metal shelf beneath the phone and thought about the taste of Ann's mouth.

"Hi, Davis, why don't you and I meet for a drink this afternoon? . . . Yeah, I know you were going to see Ann tonight, but I want to talk to you first. As soon as you get off work. It won't take long, but it's important. . . . Five? Give me that address again. Great. See you then." He hung up, leaving his hand on the receiver for a long, pensive time. His head was bent as he meditatively made his way back to the car.

Allison arrived at the condo and donned her "Ann" disguise. Davis called to say he was going to be late for their dinner date. She needed to go to the hospital to see Ann, but when she called, Ann told her not to bother.

"I'm fine. Wonderful in fact. The doctor examined me this afternoon and said the bandages could come off tomorrow. Allison, you should see me. My new boobs are gorgeous!"

"Congratulations," Allison said perfunctorily. "Does that mean I can go back to being myself tomorrow?"

"Yes. By tomorrow afternoon I'll be ready to leave the clinic. The official unveiling will be tomorrow evening."

Allison sighed in relief. "Good. You're sure you don't need anything tonight?"

"No. Just give Davis a kiss for me."

"Very funny."

She hung up, feeling no better about the situation. She still had twenty-four hours to go and couldn't shrug off the feeling of apprehension that had plagued her since Spencer's visit to the lab. A lot could go wrong in twenty-four hours.

Nine o'clock came and went and still Davis hadn't shown. She paced from sofa to window until she saw him drive up. Her relief died an instant death when she opened the front door to greet him. He was weaving his drunken way up the sidewalk, blubbering like a baby.

When he saw her on the porch, his face crumpled and he staggered toward her, launching himself against her with an impetus that almost knocked her down. He flung uncoordinated arms around her and collapsed heavily against her breasts.

"Annie, Annie," he sobbed. "How could you do it? How could you throw away the love we have for a ladies' man like Spencer?"

CHAPTER FIVE

Oh, my God," Allison groaned. How had this thing gotten so out of hand? In view of several curious neighbors, she was holding her sister's fiancé in her arms while he bawled like a baby. A week ago, she wouldn't have believed any of this was possible.

Because her knees were about to buckle under his weight and because she didn't want Ann's reputation to be jeopardized, she dragged Davis inside and collapsed with him onto the couch.

"Davis, Davis," she crooned, "she—"

Allison bit back the words she was about to say. She had already wreaked havoc on Ann's relationship with Davis. The deception only had to last one more day. Why not see it through to the bitter end? In the meantime, maybe she could rectify the damage that had been done.

"Davis, listen to me," she said firmly, trying to lift his head from her breasts.

He only clung tighter. "Annie, I love you," he mumbled drunkenly. "How could you do this to me? To us? I thought you loved me."

"I do." This time she managed to prize his head up. Brushing back the damp hair that lay plastered to his forehead, she whispered, "I love you with all my heart, darling." She kissed his lips softly and rubbed her nose against his clammy cheek. "Tell me what all this is about."

He struggled to sit up, tottering on the edge of the sofa cushions. With balled fists, he wiped the tears from his eyes. Allison was touched. He truly loved Ann.

"You say you love me? And still want to marry me?"

"Of course."

Davis licked his lips and blinked his eyes in misapprehension. "But he said—"

"Who said?"

"Spencer."

Her lips compressed in outrage. The unmitigated nerve of the man! "What did he tell you?"

"We met for a drink. I'm stinking drunk, aren't I?" he asked contritely.

She smoothed a hand from the crown of his head down to the base of his neck. "I forgive you this time. Go on. What did Spencer say?"

His lips began to tremble again. "That the two of you . . . you know, had been attracted to each other right off. I could believe that. I mean, Spencer's a good-looking guy. Since we were in grade school, the girls have flocked around him."

"So you see, there's nothing to it. I was being friendly to him and, like any egomaniac, he took it as a come-on."

"But he said that you have kissed him several times. Did you, Annie?"

Spencer Raft had no heart, no soul, no conscience. How could he hurt his friend this way? Not wanting a lie to fester between Ann and Davis, she gazed into Davis's bleak eyes as she answered, "Yes. But it meant nothing."

"He said you responded to him more passionately than any woman he's ever kissed. And that he wanted to make love to you more than any woman he's ever met." Davis buried his face in his hands, shaking his head miserably. "I couldn't believe it. I kept drinking even after he left. But I had to see you. I had to hear you say that you didn't love me anymore, that you wanted Spencer instead."

Her chest was so tight and full she could barely draw breath. A hot blush flooded not only her face but her entire body. She was the most passionate woman Spencer had ever kissed? He wanted her more than any other woman? She would have loved to indulge herself and dwell on that, but Davis looked so abject that she couldn't even think about what Spencer's words meant in relation to her. She had to straighten out the mess she had made at Ann's expense.

She clamped her hands on Davis's shoulders and pressed hard until he dropped his hands from his face and raised his soulful eyes to hers. "Spencer *is* charming and attractive. I *did* kiss him. But it meant no more to me than kissing a pretty photograph. The man is shallow, without substance. I could never love anyone else but you, Davis. Forgive me this one little transgression." Of course when he found out about the twins' switch, Ann would be totally blameless. "I want to marry you and live in the house you chose for us."

"Why are you lying to him like that, Ann?"

They both jumped at the intruding voice. It was soft, husky, throaty, but it could have been a cannon blast for all the impact it had on them. Allison bolted off the couch. Davis, still not completely sober, tumbled backward onto the floor. He righted himself with as much dignity as he could muster and stood, reeling, next to Allison.

"Get out of here," she said coldly. "You've almost ruined our life together."

Spencer was standing by the door she had failed to close when she heaved the inebriated Davis inside. He looked tall and threatening, save for the bouquet of roses he held in his hand. His dark brows were scowling in displeasure over "Ann's" profession of love and devotion to Davis.

"I'm not leaving until this is resolved."

"It *is* resolved," she declared sternly, at the same time trying to hold Davis upright. He was finding it difficult to stand, much less stand with any degree of poise. "I love Davis and I'm marrying him and I'll ask you not to interfere in our private lives again. How could you hurt him this way?"

"How could *I*?" he barked. "How could *you*? Wasn't it kinder for me to go to him, confront him man-to-man, explain the situation, rather than pretend that the kiss yesterday and the one here that first night never happened?"

Davis swayed toward Allison. "You kissed him here too? The first night you met him?" He slumped onto the couch, moaning and cradling his face once more between his hands.

She knelt in front of him. "Davis, darling, don't, please. I can't bear to see you this way. Please stop crying."

Spencer crossed the room to stand behind her, laying a comforting hand on her shoulder. "Ann, let him pour it out. In the long run it'll be easier on him."

She surged to her feet. "Will you shut up! You're a heartless bastard. Look what a mess you've made of things."

His chin thrust out belligerently. "Maybe my appearance on the scene started the mess, but you've perpetuated it. Face up to it, Ann. You've got to choose between us."

"Oh, Annie, Annie," Davis groaned. "How could you? He's not for you."

Allison's body went ramrod straight as she opened her mouth and screamed. Her arms were so stiff at her sides they could have been tied down. She wheeled around and goose-stepped away from the two men. Her eyes, teeth, and fists were all clenched as tight as she could get them in an effort to hold in the red-haired temper that rarely erupted. But when it did, it was fearsome.

Her efforts were to no avail. She blew.

Spinning around, she lunged toward Davis, who was slouched in a sodden heap on the sofa. Gripping the front of his shirt, she hauled him to his feet. That he outweighed her by seventy-five pounds seemed to make no difference. She slapped him smartly on both cheeks. "Sober up, now!" she shouted at him. "And for godsakes stop that infernal blubbering."

"You!" She turned on a dismayed Spencer and speared his belly with an imperious index finger. "You're coming with us." She reached for her purse and keys on the coffee table.

"Where?"

"Just move!" She shoved him toward the front door, dragging a stunned Davis behind her. "Get in my car," she told Spencer as she slammed the door behind them. To hell with the peering neighbors, she thought. This was all Ann's fault in the first place.

She tucked Davis into the front seat and glared up at Spencer until he submissively climbed into the back. Mercilessly she ground the ignition on Ann's car, jerked it into gear, and sped out the driveway. Her jaw worked furiously as she drove them to the clinic. Her passengers were wise enough not to initiate conversation.

The clinic wasn't too far from Ann's condo. They reached it within ten minutes. She had shaved five minutes off the trip by disregarding both the speed limit and safety.

"Whad'er we doin' here?" Davis mumbled.

"Get out. We're going inside."

When they were all three out of the car, she took Davis's arm and half dragged, half carried him to the subtly lit entrance. She let Spencer fend for himself.

The clinic's locked door infuriated her. She pounded on the plate glass with doubled fists. "Open up!" she shouted.

"Ann—" Spencer ventured bravely.

"I told you to shut up," she said over her shoulder.

A disconcerted nurse came hustling down the hall to

check on the commotion. She unlocked the door and opened it a fraction of an inch. "I'm sorry, visiting hours are over. Our patients are sleeping. Come back—"

"I'm coming in now," Allison said, pushing the nurse aside and wedging through the door, Davis in tow. "And these men are coming in with me."

"Excuse us," Spencer said politely as he passed the gape-mouthed nurse. "She's upset," he said as though that should explain everything.

Allison marched to Ann's room and shoved open the door. She switched on the light and gave Davis's shoulders a hard push. He stumbled into the room just as Ann came awake and sat up, blinking her eyes against the light.

"What's going on?" she asked. "Davis? What are you doing here? Allison?"

"Allison?" both men chorused.

Davis focused his bloodshot eyes on the hospital patient. He recognized Ann's nightgown. "Annie?" he asked in a high, thin voice.

Ann looked at Allison accusingly. "Allison, I could kill you. I look frightful. You promised, you—"

"Be quiet! You're the cause of all this," Allison snapped.

For once in their lives, Ann backed down from her sister rather than the other way around. Her mouth, hanging open, closed with a soft click of her teeth. She'd never seen Allison's eyes so greenly bright, nor her hair bristling with such fury.

Allison pointed a finger down at the occupant of the hospital bed. "Davis, that is Ann. She's had a breast enlargement. It was to be a surprise for you. She didn't want you to know until it was all over, so she asked me to impersonate her for a few days."

Davis gawked at Ann stupidly. "A breast enlargement? You mean——"

"Yes. Are you glad?" Ann asked timidly.

His disheveled head bobbed up and down. "Yeah, sure, I'm just——"

"I can't wait for you to see——"

"Please, Ann, wait until you're alone," Allison interrupted. "Unless you want Spenc——" She stepped aside so Ann could see the man standing behind her. "Ann, this is Spencer Raft, Davis's best friend," she said, sneering. Yanking the roses——by now slightly wilted——out of his hand, she tossed them unceremoniously onto the bed. "These are for you. He wants to sleep with you, by the way."

"What?" Ann exclaimed, sitting up straighter and bracing her hands behind her. Slack-jawed, Davis gazed at her breasts, which were noticeably larger even hidden behind the loose gown.

"Just because he's kissed you a few times, he thinks you're ready to break your engagement with Davis and run off with him. Oh, by the way, here's your ring back."

"But I never——" Ann began.

"How do you do, Ann," Spencer said, halting her words.

She pulled the sheet higher in a sudden rush of modesty. "Hello. It's nice to meet you."

"Likewise."

Allison sighed in exasperation. "Can I finish so I can leave?" She turned to Spencer. "I'm the one who fell down on the sidewalk, bled on you, spilled wine on you. When I fell, I lost a contact, so not only was I clumsy, I was blind, drinking from two glasses, et cetera. I'm also the one you came to see in the lab today and who spat coffee on you."

"You fell down? Where? When?" Ann asked in bewilderment. "Allison, what's going on?"

"I'm trying to explain. Spencer wants you. He thinks you don't love Davis because he's been watching *me* with him all week and apparently I'm a lousy actress."

"You mean I've been kissing—" Davis seemed to come out of his stupor and looked guiltily at Allison. "Allison, I, uh . . ." His pallid cheeks sprouted blooms of vivid color. "Annie, I kissed her, but I thought—"

"I understand, darling," Ann said, patting his hand. "This was my idea. Come sit by me. I've missed you." She reached for him and he sat on the edge of the bed, taking her hands and bringing them to his lips.

"As I was saying," Allison said loudly over their whispered love words, "Spencer went to Davis tonight and told him that you wanted him as much as he wanted you. Then Davis got drunk, thinking you were jilting him to have an affair with this philanderer. Davis came crying to me, actually to you, begging you not to throw your love away. Spencer showed up, angry that you were staying with Davis. You have to choose between them."

She drew a deep breath. "There. I think that covers all the pertinent facts and brings you up-to-date. As of this second, I'm out of it. I leave the three of you to sort it out."

Red hair flung back, spine straight and shoulders squared, she stalked from the room.

•   •   •

Her defiance lasted until she let herself into her own small apartment, musty and stifling after several days of vacancy. Then the enormity of everything that had happened avalanched on her and she fell onto the bed in a flood of tears.

She cried hard for several minutes, until the tears abated and the wracking sobs tapered off from sheer exhaustion.

Why was she crying? Wasn't she glad it was over?

She rolled to her back and let her forlorn gaze drift around the room. She had liked this apartment because it was small and compact. But after a few days in Ann's condo, its size seemed to press in on her like a shrinking jail cell.

It was neat to a fault. Nothing was ever out of place. It was as uncluttered as her heart. There was never a man's tennis sweater left on the back of a chair, or the sports section of the newspaper littering the floor. There was only one glass left in the kitchen sink, never two. Ann's house looked lived in. Allison's was as sterile as her lab. As sterile as her life.

"Stop feeling sorry for yourself," she muttered as she came off the bed and went into the bathroom. It had been her choice to make her life exactly as it was. Ann had gone to dances and parties during college. Allison had stayed home and studied. Ann had always surrounded herself with eligible men. Allison avoided social occasions. Ann was just as intelligent as Allison, but she directed it into various interests. Allison funneled hers exclusively into her work. She had often resented Ann's wasted mental powers.

But were they wasted? Ann was happy. Allison was . . . what? Resigned? Happy certainly wasn't a descriptive word that came to mind.

Up until a few days ago she had been satisfied with her life. Now, she felt a restlessness that irritated her. What did she want?

Switching out the light, she climbed into her narrow single bed. She'd gotten used to Ann's queen-sized one, bought no doubt to accommodate two people instead of one.

She'd also gotten used to pretty clothes and makeup. She'd begun to enjoy the feel of her hair swaying against her shoulders and the scent of perfume on her skin.

It alarmed her to realize just how much she would miss those feminine accoutrements. It alarmed her even more to realize how much she would miss a man's presence. His scent. His touch. His kisses. Tears collected in her eyes again.

Lord! Could she really be crying over a man? *That* man?

He had kissed and declared his desire for Ann, not Allison. He hadn't even recognized her as the woman his mouth and hands had been intimate with. He was a playboy, a jet-setter—here today, gone tomorrow—with thoughts and feelings for no one but himself. It would have been better if he'd never come to Atlanta. He wasn't for Ann. He certainly wasn't for Allison. It was a blessing that she would never see him again.

Then why did she feel more desolate than she ever had in her life?

•　　　•　　　•

"Come on, Rasputin. That's a good boy. You're such a handsome fellow. I know I'm not your ladylove, but I'll have to do. Doesn't that feel good? Hm?"

"It certainly sounds like it feels good."

With her hand still in the rabbit's cage, still bent over in a most unladylike position, Allison swiveled her head around to see Spencer standing not a yard away from her.

"What are you doing here?"

"What are you doing there?" He nodded toward the cage.

She removed her hand, patted Rasputin once, and closed the wire door. On her hand was a rabbit-fur glove. Spencer was staring at it curiously. There was a teasing gleam in his eyes and a smirk on his lips. That he was totally in control and self-assured vexed her, especially after the hellish night she'd spent weeping over him.

Her chin went up a notch. "I'm rubbing his tummy with this fur glove."

"Any particular reason why?"

"I need a seminal sample. This gets him excited."

The twinkle in his eyes flared into something else entirely. "You want excitement? Rub my tummy with it."

It was that voice, that damn husky male voice, as much as what he said that made her go weak all over. But not wanting to give him an inch, knowing well he could turn it into a mile, she angrily jerked the glove off and flung it down. "Sorry, Rasputin. I'll have to get back to you later," she muttered as she put needed space between Spencer and herself. She rounded on him when she was a safe distance away. "I've had all of you I'm going to take, Mr. Raft."

He grinned at her with unrepentant arrogance. "No, you haven't. You'll be taking a whole lot more of me."

Fury and desire warred within her. Even as she closed her mind to the insinuating, evocative words he spoke, her body responded to them. "I'm sick of your crude innuendos. Playing my sister, I had to put up with them in order to keep peace with Davis. But speaking for myself now, I think you're disgusting."

"I think you're spectacular."

A sob heaved in her chest and she turned away before he could see. "Stop mocking me." She had always thought him conceited and selfish. But she hadn't expected deliberate cruelty from him.

"Mocking you?" He quickly came up behind her and laid his hands on her shoulders. When he tried to turn her to face him, she resisted and shrugged off his hands.

"I'm sure you all had a good laugh last night after I left the clinic." Were his fingers lightly caressing the back of her neck or was that her imagination?

"I don't remember any belly laughs. Davis and I filled in a few gaps in your story. Ann was dismayed by all that had happened and commiserated with you. She tried to call and apologize."

"I took my phone off the hook." Finally squirming free of his hands, she went to the window and toyed with the cord on the blinds, keeping her back to him. "I didn't want to talk to anybody, not even Ann. I hope she got her money's worth out of that operation after the hell she's put me through."

"Were her breasts the same as yours?"

She glanced at him sharply. He was close again. Too

close. And looking at her as if he'd already succeeded in getting her into his bed and was well acquainted with her body. She could no more keep from answering him than she could stop her heart from beating. "Identical."

His eyes drifted down to her breasts, lingered an audaciously long time, then coasted back up to her face. "Why did she bother?" For several ponderous moments they simply stared at each other.

Allison became lost in his blue eyes. Their heat seemed to swirl around her, warming her body, making it pliant and yearning. She liked the rough texture of his skin and the thick luxury of his brows. She even liked the creases and lines in his face, which were a shade lighter than the tanned planes. Her fingertips longed to examine each one.

But she roused herself out of the daze and moved away.

He spoke first. "Ann teased Davis about kissing you. He was mortified that he'd treated you like his fiancée. I don't think he'll be able to look you in the eye for a long time."

She had migrated to one of the high slab tables where microscopes, Bunsen burners, and beakers were ready for use. She put her eye to a microscope, knowing full well there was no slide beneath it. From the corner of her eye, she saw Spencer sit down on the stool close to her. When he hitched his heel over the lowest rung, his bent knee bumped against her thigh. She shifted away.

"What were you doing all this time that Davis was being embarrassed and Ann was teasing him?"

"Me? I was feeling a great sense of relief that I wouldn't have to sacrifice my friendship with Davis for the woman I want."

She snapped to attention and faced him, somehow placing herself in the danger zone between his wide-spread thighs. "What did you say? Don't you understand? Ann is in love with Davis. She's going to marry him. She only met you last night."

"*I* understand. I don't think you do." Somehow he managed to clasp both her arms and ease her closer to him. They were belly to belly before she even realized she had been propelled forward. "It's you I've been pursuing these last few days, Allison, not your sister. Rather than being peeved over the switch in identities, I'm delighted about it. You and I are free to continue what started the other night when I first held you."

She leaned as far away from him as his encircling arms would permit and stared at him as though he were insane. "You're not nearly as bright as I gave you credit for, Mr. Raft. Haven't you figured it out? Look at me. You danced with Ann. You kissed Ann. You touched Ann. Not me." She spread her arms wide. "This is me."

His eyes flickered over the ponytail, the pencil stuck behind her ear, the eyeglasses she'd worn because her eyes had been sandy with dried tears and the lack of sleep. They took in the lab coat, the conservative skirt, and ugly shoes.

"You're adorable. I especially like you when you're breathing flames the way you were at Davis and me last night. A regular firebrand when you lose your temper. You were fascinating and sexy. I wanted to fling you to the floor and take you right there, Davis or not."

Flabbergasted, she succeeded in wrenching herself out of his embrace and backing away from him. "You came in here yesterday, spent a half hour with me, and didn't recognize me as the woman you'd kissed only the day before."

"That's because I wasn't looking for you, Allison." He came off the stool and advanced on her. "Had I done this, I would have known you instantly."

She didn't know a man could move so fast and make it look so effortless. His mouth was pressing hotly over hers and his arms were folding tightly around her before she knew what had happened. He wasted no time, commanding her lips to open with an impatient thrust of his tongue. Swamped by his masculine appeal, she invited him inside with a low moan and acquiescent lips.

His tongue plowed through the sweet textures of her lips and mouth, sampling, tasting, swirling, stroking, probing. Her arms hung limply at her sides, but her body ignited like a torch. He rubbed his middle against hers to dispel any doubt in her mind that it was her he wanted. In response, her womanhood liquefied and flowered and molded to his hardness.

Tamping down such mounting desire was no small task, but she fought herself to do it. She'd never given a man the power to hurt her. None had ever gotten that close. She had built a wall around herself. With each kiss, Spencer was creating a chink in that wall and getting much too close to her inner self. He could and would break her heart, destroy the life she had if she let him.

With the heels of her hands on his shoulders, she pushed herself away. She drew rapid breaths, hoping he'd think they were due to rage rather than passion.

"You forget that I let you kiss me only to spare Davis embarrassment. I don't have to submit to your shabby embraces anymore."

"Shabby?"

"Yes, shabby. Now please go. I don't know why you bothered coming here today, but you're unwelcome. Don't try to see me again."

Keeping his eyes trained on her, he relented and backed away. She was the first to surrender and look away, which was as good as a confession that she was lying. And he knew it.

"You don't like me at all, is that it?"

"No. I mean, yes, that's it. I don't like you."

"Not even a little?"

The teasing, taunting lilt in his voice made her grit her teeth with aggravation. "No."

"Gee, that's too bad."

She looked up at him, wary, but curious too. "Why?"

"I came here to volunteer."

"Volunteer? For what?"

"To father the child you want to have."

"What an excellent idea!"

CHAPTER SIX

Stupefied, she stared first at Spencer, who had made the outlandish suggestion, then at Dr. Hyden, who had endorsed it from the doorway. Spencer's eyes didn't waver from Allison. Dr. Hyden was the first of the three to move. He came forward, his eyes alight with interest.

"You didn't tell me you were screening candidates," he teased Allison jovially.

She forced words up out of a constricting throat. "I'm not screening candidates for anything. I don't know where he got such a harebrained idea."

"Why, from you, I imagine," Dr. Hyden said. "You were talking to me about it only a few days ago. How do you do, young man," he said, extending his hand to Spencer. "Dirk Hyden."

Spencer shook the proffered hand heartily. "Spencer Raft. A pleasure to meet you, Dr. Hyden."

The fuse on Allison's temper had just about burned

out again. "Would you two gentlemen please get acquainted somewhere else. I have work to do." She spun around and headed for the animal cages. Spencer caught the hem of her lab coat and pulled her up short.

"Uh-uh. We're discussing a scientific experiment here. Romeo can wait."

"Rasputin," she snapped, trying unsuccessfully to work her coat from his steely grip. "I don't know anything about a scientific experiment that concerns you."

"Sure you do," Spencer went on, undaunted. "Ann told me all about it last night. She went into considerably more detail on your work than you and Davis did the other night at dinner. She said you wanted to conduct experiments on the correlation between heredity and intelligence. You told her, this week in fact, that if you found a suitable sire you'd like to have a baby to test your theories on."

How could a statement so innocently spoken ricochet so incriminatingly? "Ann was still dopey after her surgery," she exclaimed. "In answer to her question about my work, I *jokingly* said it was a shame I couldn't experiment with a human baby. That's all there was to it. I wasn't serious. I didn't literally mean that I wanted to have a baby for such a purpose."

"Why not, if you have a man volunteering to father it?"

"Yes, why not?" Dr. Hyden chimed in.

"Why not?" she gasped. Was she the only sane person left on the planet?

"I repeat that I think it's an excellent idea," Dr. Hyden said. "I told you you'd make a perfect mother. All you needed was an equally qualified father." He ignored

Allison's dismayed stare and addressed Spencer. "Please don't be offended by my questions."

"Fire away," Spencer said congenially, dropping onto the stool once more. He was at ease and, by all indications, enjoying himself immensely.

"Do you know what your I.Q. is?"

"Somewhere around a hundred and seventy I think."

Dr. Hyden's eyebrows shot up, impressed. He lowered his glasses from the top of his head and subjected Spencer to a thorough going-over. "You certainly are an impressive physical specimen. Are both your parents still living?"

"Yes."

"In good health?"

"Excellent."

"Brothers or sisters?"

"Unfortunately I'm an only child."

"No hereditary diseases in your family, I hope."

"None that I know of."

"A nice-looking fellow too." Dr. Hyden turned to Allison, who was standing with her arms folded beneath her breasts, foot tapping, fuming. "Congratulations. You've selected a perfect specimen."

"I didn't select him for anything! I'm dutifully impressed with his qualifications, but I hardly want to have a baby with every stud who has a Phi Beta Kappa key."

Dr. Hyden thoughtfully weighed her words and turned back to Spencer. He was scowling slightly. "Are you a 'stud' just out for a good time?"

"No." Spencer left the stool and, with no regard for Dr. Hyden's judgmental eyes, came to stand in front of

Allison. "I like Allison very much. I think she likes me. I want to develop a relationship with her."

"Ah, well, that's wonderful," Dr. Hyden said, beaming and rubbing his hands together.

"But she's stubborn," Spencer continued. "She's resisting the idea of our being together."

Dr. Hyden frowned at his protégée. "Yes, I've known her to be stubborn." Allison remained sullen and silent. But the hot gleam in Spencer's eyes as he gazed down at her restored Dr. Hyden's optimism. He clapped Spencer on the back. "I have every confidence in your ability to convince her, my boy. Allison, I'll expect periodic reports on the project. Good day to you both." He breezed out, his lab coat popping behind him like a sail.

Livid green eyes sliced up to the triumphant blue ones. "You think you're extremely clever, don't you?"

He flashed her that movie-star grin. "Dr. Hyden seems to think so."

"Well, I don't. I think you're manipulative and arrogant and insufferably vain."

"See? We balance each other because you're far too self-effacing and humble."

Seething, she turned her back on him and pretended to go about her work. Her busy motions didn't deter him. Placing his hands on her shoulders, he turned her to face him, wedging her between the high table and his hard body. He lifted the glasses off her nose and set them aside.

"That proves it."

"What?" he asked as he slid the rubber band from her hair.

"That you were only attracted to me when I looked

like Ann. Why don't you stop playing this perverted game?" She tried to sound stern, but her voice quavered and there was a frantic edge to it as he ran his hands through her unbound hair. She should be struggling, fighting him. Instead she was permitting him to adjust his body to hers with breathtaking accuracy.

"This isn't a game and I intend to be only a little perverted at first."

His thumbs found the backs of her ears and massaged them as she moaned, "Leave me alone."

"I can't leave you alone, Allison," he whispered as he bent his head and laid his lips on her neck. They shifted back and forth. "I'll admit to liking your hair better loose so I can run my fingers through it. I think you look cute as a button in your glasses. I only took them off so they wouldn't get broken."

"Broken?" she asked breathlessly. His lips were toying with her ear. "What are you going to do?"

"Try to get you to admit what you already know."

Then his mouth found hers. Lightly at first, his lips caressed, touching softly, retreating, touching again. His tongue flicked over her lips, dampening them and making them hungry for his taste. "Pay attention now and let me show you how it will be with us," he said against her lips.

His tongue sank deeply into her mouth, and still it reached, reached for more of her. He moved his head from one side to the other, slowly, savoringly, as his tongue slid back and forth over hers, mating.

Her breasts were flattened against his chest, but they plumped at the sides. The backs of his knuckles found those sweet curves and moved up and down over them.

Even through her lab coat, blouse, and bra she could feel
the caress. Then one hand moved to the small of her back
and pressed her closer, his alerted virility gently grinding
against the cleft of her thighs.

By the time he lifted his lips from hers, she was as
warm and flexible as wax. "We'd make a wonderful baby,"
he murmured, lifting the dew of their kiss off her lips with
the agile tip of his tongue. "Think about it, and I'll pick you
up at eight tonight. I'll expect your answer over dinner."

She almost collapsed like a ragdoll when he released
her. It was long after he left the lab that her heart stopped
pounding, her respiration slowed, and she was able to
pull herself together.

Why not? Why not? Why not?

"Why not?" she said to the mirror on the back of her
closet door. "A million reasons why not, that's why not."

Her only appropriate dress still didn't have the flair of
anything in Ann's wardrobe, but it would have to do.
The soft blue georgette with the neatly pleated bodice
made her look like exactly what she was, an old maid.

What do you care what you look like for him?

All right, you care. But only a little. You just don't
want him to think you're a desperate spinster.

But back to the baby. Baby? Are you really thinking
about this? Yes, because he'll expect an answer and you'd
better have myriad reasons why it's out of the question.
He's so damn clever and glib.

One, you don't even like him.

But he won't be around after it's done. You'll only be
using his . . . his . . . seed. (What an Old Testament word

for a scientist to be using!) It really doesn't matter if you like him or not. You have to agree with Dr. Hyden that if you were to choose a father for your child, Spencer Raft would be a good choice.

Two, having a child without having a husband. That's hardly a valid argument in this day and age. Thousands of single women raise children alone, single men as well.

But what about your parents? They would be shocked that their brainy Allison, who seemingly cared for no living creature outside her lab, would have a baby out of wedlock. Another Biblical allusion.

What do you care what anyone thinks, even your parents? You would be doing this for you, wouldn't you? She turned away from the mirror and let her gaze travel over the empty apartment. Yes, for me. This would be my baby. My child. Someone to love me and for me to love back.

Reason number three . . .

She found a tube of mascara in the back of a drawer. It was dried out, but a little water mixed in produced enough for her to color the tips of her lashes. She wore the pearl earrings her mother had given her last Christmas for the first time. She wound her hair into a bun, but a looser version of the one she usually wore. There were soft tendrils clinging to the base of her neck and framing her cheeks. Checking her image in the mirror one last time, she was rather proud of the results of her efforts.

But when the doorbell rang, she jumped and her palms were instantly slick with sweat. Her reasons why they couldn't parent a child hadn't stood up against her own arguments. They would surely perish under Spencer's dissection.

"Damn him for doing this to me," she muttered as she switched out the light in her bedroom and headed for the front door.

For long seconds after she opened the door, the only part of him that moved was his eyes. They scaled her, painting hot ribbons of sensation from the top of her head to the tips of her toes.

"You look beautiful, Allison." Stepping into the room, he took her hand and lifted it to his mouth. He turned it over and pressed his lips to the back of her wrist and the accelerating pulse that beat there. Then he kissed her mouth with soft tenderness.

"You look nice too," she said shakily when he released her. He had on a double-breasted navy blazer, oyster-colored slacks, and a cream-colored shirt. He was tieless. The shirt's collar was opened to reveal a tanned throat and the top of a deep chest forested with crisply curling dark hair. There was a jaunty red silk handkerchief in the breast pocket of the blazer. "You look ready to heave anchor and sail away."

He slid his fingers down her cheek and onto her throat. "Not yet, I'm not."

Deep in her body, butterflies were dancing. One fluttered up to her throat as she tried to speak. "Are you ready to go?"

"I'd like to see your apartment."

"There's nothing to see." She made a sweep of her arm, indicating the small living room and a kitchen beyond a separating bar. "This is it."

He glanced at it, but made no comment. When his eyes came back to hers, they were void of expression. "Let's go then. Do you have a wrap?"

"No."

They made their way down the exterior stairs. She jumped nervously when he closed his hand around the back of her neck. His fingers were hard, callused, but gentle on her skin. At the car, he held the door for her. When he got in, he refrained from turning the key. After several seconds, Allison, sitting as stiff and wooden as a tobacco-store Indian, glanced across the interior of the car.

"What's wrong?" she asked.

"That's what I'd like to know."

"I don't know what you mean."

"Every time I touch you, you jump like you're frightened of me. It bugs the hell out of me and I want you to stop it right here and now. I'm not going to rape you, Allison. I've never had to force my attentions on a woman, so will you please stop acting like you're going to be my first victim?"

Her eyes skittered away. "I didn't know I was doing that."

"Well, you are. Believe me, when I get ready to make love to you, you'll be the first to know." Her eyes flew back to his. "If I'd wanted to make love to you before dinner, we'd be in your bedroom by now. I'd already have your dress, slip, bra, and pantyhose off and you'd be lying beneath me, naked. I'd be kissing you and stroking your breasts and thighs, and you'd be reaching for me and I'd be ready." He let that sink in while he kept her mesmerized with an intense stare. "But until that time will you relax?"

Relax? When he had just itemized every garment she had on under her dress as though he had X-ray vision?

When he had just detailed foreplay in a most explicit way? But she nodded her head anyway, just so he'd start the car and stop looking at her with a penetration she could feel.

Oddly enough, as soon as they were on their way, he engaged her in light conversation. They talked about everything and nothing. He asked if she had talked to Ann that day.

"Yes, when I got home I phoned her. She was already back in her condo and cooking a big celebration dinner for Davis. She seemed to be feeling fine."

"That was a crazy thing she did," Spencer said, laughing. "I hope Davis is pleased."

"I'm sure he will be." They smiled at each other and Allison realized that she *was* relaxed.

He placed his hand on the back of her waist as he escorted her into the restaurant and smiled down at her when she didn't flinch. All through dinner, he seemed determined to put her at ease. There were even a few times when she burst into spontaneous laughter. It wasn't until their dessert was served that he broached the subject that had been deliberately shoved into the background all evening.

He sipped his coffee and carefully replaced the cup in the saucer. "Have you thought about our project?"

To keep from dropping her spoon, she dipped it into the remaining chocolate mousse. Before, it had been rich and creamy and cool. Now it suddenly went tasteless on her tongue. "Yes."

"And?"

"There are all kinds of complications involved, besides just the obvious."

"Let me try to clear up some ambiguities." He moved his cup and saucer aside and, folding his arms on the table, leaned closer to her. "First, I don't want you to worry about the financial aspects. I'll certainly provide for the child before and after he arrives."

"I wouldn't ask."

He gave her a withering look. "Yeah, I know, you proud, stubborn redhead. That's why I insist. Now be quiet and let me finish. Second, how do you intend to deliver?"

She couldn't believe that she was actually participating in this conversation, but she answered nonetheless. "Natural childbirth, if there are no complications."

"Good. I want to be a part of that."

Her eyes rounded. "You do?" She hadn't counted on sharing the experience of birth with him. That seemed dangerously intimate, something two people in love should share.

"I do." His teeth shone up whitely in his dark face as he smiled. "Don't you think I'd be interested in the birth of my own child?"

"I suppose so." She contemplated the pattern of the sterling for a moment before asking softly, "Spencer, why—"

"Say it again."

"Pardon?"

"Say my name again. That's the first time you've said it."

"I've said it many times."

"Not as Allison, you haven't."

He was staring at her mouth so intently that she wet her lips with her tongue to cool them. They seemed to burn under the heat of his eyes. "Spencer, I find this whole thing bizarre. Why do you want to do it?"

"Would you believe me if I said it was a way to win your heart?"

"No."

"I didn't think so. Let's just say, I'm doing it for the furtherance of science."

She couldn't look at him as she asked the next question. "Do you . . . Have you . . . Would this child be your first?"

He took her hand and clasped it between both of his until she looked up at him. "Yes. My first and only. And I would want to see him often. I want it agreed upon beforehand that there would be no future legal battles to say that I couldn't."

"Of course not. I would always want what is best for the child. He should know his father." She really didn't think that a man with Spencer's wanderlust would remain underfoot and interfere in the upbringing of the child. The newness would soon wear off. If the child ever saw him, it would be infrequently. That was an easy condition to agree to.

"You speak of the child as a boy," she observed. "Will it matter to you if it's a girl?"

"Not at all. I rather fancy having a red-haired daughter." She was ready with a shy smile, but his next question left her with a blank face and nothing to say. "Do you plan to breast-feed?"

She'd never known that the base of her fingers were erotically sensitive. But Spencer's thumb was raking along that ridge where her fingers joined her hand, rising and dipping to follow the scalloped line. Sensation after sensation rippled through her. Or was it the way his eyes were scouring her breasts that made her feel marshy on the inside? Or was it the mental image of her nursing a child—a dark-haired, blue-eyed child—while Spencer gazed on adoringly, reaching to touch her milk-laden breast with the fingers that were eliciting such wanton tingles in her womanhood even now?

"I'd definitely try breast-feeding," she said scratchily.

"Good. I approve." His eyes were hooded and smoky. The expression on his face was personal and private, the same he wore in her vision. It said he wanted to be next to taste her breast, next to suck at that marbleized nipple. "When will you be fertile?"

It was a perfectly scientific and necessary question. Yet following on the heels of her daydream, it sent a trill of sensation feathering its way up from her thighs to the back of her throat, tapping each erogenous spot on its way. Flustered, she lowered her eyes. She, who dealt with fertility and reproduction every day, was feeling as awkward discussing it as a Victorian maiden.

"Later this week," she said in a hoarse whisper. "But there's no rush."

"I think the sooner the better, don't you?"

"I suppose. But of course it can be done anytime once I have the . . . uh . . . specimen from you."

"Specimen?"

"Yes. It freezes."

He squinted one eye closed and cocked his head to one side. "I think I missed something. What freezes?"

She glanced up at him, but immediately her eyes fell away again. "The, uh, you know. The semen."

"Freezes!" He burst out laughing, capturing the

attention of diners at surrounding tables. Allison shifted nervously in her chair.

"Everyone is looking," she said under her breath.

He leaned closer, trying to suppress his laughter. "You're talking about artificial insemination?"

"Yes, and please lower your voice."

Instead he laughed again, hard and gustily. When at last his mirth subsided, he said in a low, confidential voice, "Miss Leamon, understand this. Nothing of mine gets frozen. Rumplestiltskin might be satisfied with a fur glove getting the job done, but I assure you I am not."

Her blush was so fiery, the roots of her hair seemed to ignite. "The rabbit's name is *Rasputin* and I hope you don't mean what I think you mean."

"Test your theory."

She leaned forward now and hissed, "You had another way of fertilization in mind?"

He grinned broadly. "The conventional way, yes."

"B—but I can't do it the conventional way!"

"No problem. We'll do it in any position you like. I'm versatile, willing to try—"

"Will you stop! I meant us"—her hand rapidly sawed between the two of them—"us together at all is impossible."

"Why?"

"Because the only reason we're discussing this in the first place is strictly to produce another human being. All I need is a specimen from you and I can try impregnation again and again until it takes."

His eyes slid over her seductively. "That doesn't preclude my method. I rather like the idea of it requiring lots of tries." Before she could bolt from her chair, he trapped her hand in his. "Why are you so surprised? I told you yesterday what I wanted. I said frankly that I wanted to take you to bed."

"You said that about Ann."

"Dammit, I hadn't even met Ann when I said that!" He was really angry. His fingers squeezed hers and his mouth had thinned to a hard line.

"Well, I don't want to go to bed with you for any reason."

"Liar."

"I don't!"

"Yes, you do. *And* you want that child."

She had to try a different tack. This one obviously wasn't working. "You expect me to believe that you want to make a baby with a woman who fell flat on her face on the sidewalk, went through an entire evening blinded because she lost her contact, fumbled and stumbled and——"

"I came after you, didn't I? Now stop all this foolishness and give me an answer, yea or nay?"

She gnawed on her lower lip. "I don't know. I was thinking about it the other way. It never occurred to me that you would stoop so low as to demand this."

"You'd be surprised how far I'll go to get what I want," he said, signaling the waiter for their check. "Think about it. Take your time. I'll give you till we get to your apartment."

They drove home in silence. Only once did he speak to her.

"Are you thinking about it?"

"Yes. Be quiet."

At her door, she took a deep breath and turned to

face him. "All right. I want that baby. He'll be important to my work and important to my life. Since no other men with your qualifications are waiting in the wings and since you're willing, I agree to let you father him."

"On my terms?" His voice caressed her as significantly as his lips were caressing her earlobe.

She swallowed. "Yes. On your terms. Though I think you're an unscrupulous blackmailer."

He caught her lobe between his teeth and worried it gently as he chuckled. "Is that any way to talk about the father of your child?"

"I'll call you later in the week when it's time," she said breathlessly. His tongue was a warm, wet playful thing against her neck.

"No way."

She wormed her way out of the circle of his arms. "What do you mean, 'no way'?"

"We're human beings creating another human being. We're not laboratory animals conditioned to perform when the time is right, though I wouldn't object if you brought that fur glove along."

"Brought it along where?"

"We're going to Hilton Head and stay on my boat alone together."

Once again he had pulled the rug out from under her. "But I can't just pack up and go away with you."

"I'm sure one call to Dr. Hyden will clear you at work. Leave that to me. You just be ready tomorrow at noon. It takes several hours by car and there's no better time to arrive at Hilton Head than at sunset."

"But—"

"Don't bring any charts or thermometers or anything clinical. We'll isolate ourselves on the yacht and do what comes naturally when the time seems natural to do it."

"Who's the scientist, me or you?"

"Don't pack a lot of clothes either. You won't need them. Now let's do a practice run."

"Practice run?"

He cradled her face between his palms and kissed each feature. Starting with her temple, his lips softly worked their way across her forehead. He kissed each eyelid, then her cheekbones in turn. He even dropped quick, funny kisses on her nose. He kissed her chin. Then her mouth.

His lips opened over hers possessively, and she gave no thought to not parting hers. His tongue slid along her lower lip, testing and tasting.

"Spencer," she cried softly.

"Hm?"

"That tickles."

His laugh was soft puffs of air against her lips. "Does it?"

He sampled the sleek inner lining of her lips. He dragged his tongue along the rows of straight white teeth, then pushed it into the silky hollow of her mouth.

His arms closed around her tightly. He snuggled his body against hers, unable to get close enough. She didn't know what to do with her arms and hands, so she tentatively rested them on his shoulders.

"I want to touch you tonight," he rasped as one hand worked its way between their bodies and began undoing the buttons of her dress.

I should stop this, her mind screamed, but her body was unwilling to listen. Her breasts ached for his touch. It was insanity, but she was weary of always being sane.

When all the buttons were unfastened, he slid his hand into her bodice and covered the swell of her breast with his palm. He pressed it lovingly. "Oh, you feel so good," he said against her lips. "Soft and full, perfect. I can't wait to see you. Kiss you here."

He took her mouth again, making love to it with his tongue while his thumb stroked her nipple to a tight bead of desire. Then the other breast was treated to the same sensual torment.

An ache grew inside her, winding tighter and tighter, until she thought she'd die a glorious death from the pressure. Why had she denied herself this? Why had she deluded herself into thinking that human sexuality was purely mechanical and physical? It wasn't. Her soul yearned for fulfillment as much as her body craved it.

When Spencer's hand glided over her slip, down her rib cage, over her belly, and touched the point of her delta, she uttered a strangled cry and clutched at him shamefully.

"I know, I know," he whispered urgently in her ear, his breath hot and fervent. He removed his hand and cupped her chin with it. "I want to be inside you so bad I can't stand it, but I want everything to be perfect the first time."

Gradually he pulled away from her. Her cheeks were fevered with arousal and shame. From the first moment she had seen him, this man had exercised some strange power over her. Around him she didn't recognize herself.

He rebuttoned her dress, then tilted her head up with a finger beneath her chin. "Are you all right?"

"I think so," she said with a shaky smile.

"You'll be ready to go tomorrow at noon?"

"I'll be ready."

She let herself into her apartment. Switching on the light in the bedroom and dropping her purse onto the bed, she went to the mirror on the closet door. For long minutes, she stared at herself. Her eyes were bright and shiny, clear and steadfast, transmitting a truth she could no longer ignore.

She was going away with him tomorrow. And it wasn't because it was time for her to throw caution aside and have an affair. It wasn't for the sake of science. It wasn't even to produce a child who would give her life purpose.

It was because she loved Spencer Raft.

CHAPTER SEVEN

Admitting that she loved him wasn't something she took lightly. How many other women had succumbed to his charm? No doubt he'd left a chain of broken hearts around the world. Allison would only be another link.

He certainly didn't love her, but he desired her. For some puzzling reason, he had found her attractive enough to pursue. Had her lack of sophistication attracted him? Maybe that in itself made her a desirable novelty.

She was going into the affair with both eyes open. She wasn't deceiving herself as to the nature of his feelings for her. He was an adventurer and philanderer. He would leave soon. If she became pregnant, she would see him periodically when he visited the child. Never would she make herself a millstone around his neck. But she would have a living part of him with her always, the child.

If there was no child, she would still have a memory to fill the loneliness of her life, to light the dim hours. Allison Leamon needed recollections of one time in her life when she had known love and affection from a man. She desperately needed that.

So she was going to Hilton Head with no hesitation. If there were regrets later, she'd cope with them then.

She was awakened early by her telephone. "Hello."

"I can't believe it! I simply can't believe it!"

Shaking the muzziness from her head, Allison sat up. "Hi, Ann. What can't you believe?"

"That you're going to Hilton Head with Spencer."

"He didn't waste any time bragging about his conquest, did he?"

"Don't get defensive. He called here to tell Davis that he was leaving today. Davis pressured him to say why and when he told us, we couldn't believe it."

"You said that already. You're doing my jittery ego a world of good, Annie." Was it so unheard of that Spencer would invite her to spend a few days on his yacht? Surely he hadn't told them about the baby.

"Now there you go again, reading something into a harmless statement. I can believe that Spencer asked you, what I can't believe is that you accepted."

She sighed in relief and gratitude. He'd been enough of a gentleman not to tell them the real reason behind her going. "I think it'll be fun to get away for a few days. I've never been to Hilton Head and—"

"Allison, that's not what I want to hear about. I want to hear all the smutty details of your whirlwind love affair."

"There is no whirlwind love affair."

"To hear Spencer talk about it, there is. When he finally broke down and told Davis that you were going with him, he went on and on about how beautiful you are, how he'd been swept off his feet the first time he saw you. By the way, remind me to get mad as hell at you later for not telling me about all this as it was happening. I missed all the excitement. Anyway"—she paused to draw a deep breath—"I've got to hurry—"

"So do I, Annie. I have a million things to do before noon. What time is it? Oh, Lord, after nine. Bye, Ann. I'll call—"

"Just a minute. You shower and dress. I'm coming around at ten to take you shopping. We'll hit the stores as soon as they open."

"Shopping? For what?"

"For clothes suitable for an affair. Don't argue. Bye."

The next several hours passed in a blur of activity and chaos. As she drank her morning coffee, Allison made a list of things to do to secure her apartment while she was away. She showered and shampooed in a hurry and began sorting through her meager wardrobe in a frantic search for something one would wear on a yacht. When her search proved fruitless, she began to think Ann's shopping idea had been divinely inspired.

They went to the glitziest boutiques in the city. For an hour and a half, Ann drove sales clerks into a frenzy until Allison had three new slacks sets, two yummy sundresses, three frothy nightgowns, four new swimsuits, and half a dozen pairs of shorts and tops. What Allison didn't have time to try on, Ann did for her, taking into account the new fullness of her breasts.

They also stopped at the cosmetics counter of a department store for a crash course in the application of makeup from a harried cosmetologist who collapsed in nervous exhaustion after they left. Fragrance was purchased—a light, floral, airy scent that the saleslady swore was "*yours,* dear."

They beat Spencer to Allison's apartment only by a few minutes. Quickly snipping off the price tags, Ann began folding clothes into the suitcase. Allison dressed in one of her new outfits, a pair of loose beige cotton slacks with a voluminous top that draped over shoulder and thigh and was only given shape by a green fishnet belt at her waist.

"You're not taking that hideous old shirt of Daddy's, are you?"

"No. Only those sinful cobwebs you called negligees."

"Good. Did you pack all that new makeup, Allison?"

"Yes."

"Do you swear? If you get to Hilton Head and make yourself look like a frump, I'll never speak to you again."

"I packed it, I packed it and—oh, God!" she gasped, crossing her hands over her chest when the doorbell pealed. "There he is."

"Go let him in. I'll close up the suitcase," Ann offered.

At the door, Allison took a moment to catch her breath. There was nothing she could do about her thumping heart. It was amazing how a pragmatic woman like her had been caught up in Ann's romantic enthusiasm. She could almost believe this was an elopement or a honeymoon. When she opened the door, Spencer didn't dispel the mood. His blue eyes virtually stripped away her new ensemble and devoured her.

"Hi."

"Hi."

He stepped inside, but halted uncertainly when Ann came through the bedroom door. With her hair loose, makeup applied, and wearing new clothes, Allison was again a dead ringer for her twin. Spencer's eyes ping-ponged between the two women several times before he smiled, enclosed Allison in his arms, and kissed her ardently.

"Ready?" he asked when he at last freed her mouth.

Ann put her hands on her hips. Her expression was militant. "How come you could tell us apart when Davis fell for the switch hook, line, and sinker?"

They laughed at her, though Allison's laugh was half-hearted and tremulous. His kiss had ruined her for idle conversation. She hadn't known a tongue could be that limber.

"I called Dr. Hyden myself." She hoped her voice wasn't as unsettled by his kiss as the rest of her.

"I know. He said he'd talked to you."

"You called him too?"

"I wasn't going to give you any room to back out."

"I wouldn't have let her anyway," Ann said. "Her bags are ready." She tilted her head in the direction of the bedroom.

Within minutes Ann was waving them off after a swift hug and a "Don't say no to *anything*," whispered in Allison's ear. Allison found herself sitting in a car next to a man she'd met less than a week ago, on her way to his ocean-going yacht where they would be alone with only one purpose in mind . . . making love.

"I like your outfit," he said conversationally.

"Thanks."

"Is it new?"

"Yes."

"Your hair looks pretty today."

"Thanks."

"Is the air conditioner too cool?"

"No."

"Can I expect one-word responses the whole time we're away?"

She glanced at him and saw the teasing gleam in his eyes. Ducking her head self-consciously, she laughed. "I'm sorry."

"Terrific. We're making progress. That's two words." He reached across the car and laid a hand on her thigh. "Are you going to sit way over there the whole trip?"

"Where do you want me to sit?"

He applied a slight pressure to her thigh and enough of a tugging motion to let her know what she had already known without having to ask. She scooted across the seat of the car until she was close beside him, her left thigh pressing against his right. He swung an arm over her shoulders, slid his hand into the wide neck of her top, and caressed her shoulder.

"Do me a favor," he said.

"What?"

"Put your hand on my thigh."

She had expected him to say, "Check the road map," "Turn up the radio," "Lock your door." She had expected just about anything but "Put your hand on my thigh." And because she didn't have a clever comeback or put-down or argument against it, she complied.

He was wearing casual slacks, expensive but casual. They were a light bluish-gray summer-weight fabric. The cloth was soft against her palm, but the muscles of his thigh were as hard as iron. She was tempted to flex her fingers, to slide them up and down the strong column, to curl them into the inside of his leg. But her hand remained motionless once it had found a comfortable spot.

"Thanks," he growled, letting his gaze leave the road long enough so that he could nuzzle her ear.

He began telling her about his childhood, his parents, his friendship with Davis, his college days, and the sports he had participated in. His voice was lulling and she had almost become accustomed to the callused fingertips that played with her collarbone and sifted across her chest.

Then he said, "Do you know what it's doing to me to know that there's a scarce six inches between the tip of my finger and the tip of your breast?"

Her breath staggered in her throat. "Ann wouldn't let me wear a bra today."

"I don't know whether to thank her or curse her. This is torture. Sublime torture, but torture just the same."

He removed his hand. Allison had mixed emotions about that. She had loved the feel of his caress, but was frightened of what it did to her, converting her body into a sensory receptor that couldn't seem to get enough. More frightening was how she was coming to take such caresses for granted. This love affair was temporary. Not for one moment could she forget that.

With his hand now free, he lifted hers, which was still lying on his thigh, to his lips. He kissed her palm, twirling his tongue against the sensitive flesh with an intimate caress she felt in the pit of her stomach. Then he returned her hand, higher on his thigh this time, and pressed his hand over it.

They traveled leisurely, stopping when the mood struck them. They shared a Coke and a bag of peanuts at one rest stop, an ice cream cone at another. They licked the cone, kissed. Licked, kissed. Until it got all jumbled up and out of sequence. Laughing, he blotted her chin with a paper napkin when a chocolate chip got misplaced.

She told him anecdotes of Ann and her as children and the confusion they had often caused. She tried to explain the deep and abiding relationship that existed between twins. She also confessed some of the drawbacks to being one.

"It's like I'm not complete, that maybe Ann's got an essential part of me inside her and I'll never have it." Glancing at him timidly, she asked, "Does that sound crazy?"

"No. But I haven't noticed any deficiencies in you. You're a self-contained woman and I can't think of anything Ann has that you lack."

Lightening the mood, he regaled her with stories of people he had met abroad.

But whatever they were doing, he was touching her. Somewhere, somehow, his hands were constantly on her. Allison was certain that to anyone observing them, they appeared to be a couple deeply in love. It was easy to see why Spencer had no trouble seducing women all over the world. He was expert at it. Instinctively he treated a woman just as she wanted to be treated. He made Allison feel sexy, alluring, beautiful, witty, captivating, when actually it was she who was being captivated.

The closer they got to the ocean, the flatter the land became and the higher the humidity. Curly gray moss draped from the branches of massive oak trees, flowers bloomed in lush profusion, pine trees speared skyward. They crossed the state line from northern Georgia into South Carolina and a few miles beyond came to the causeway that led onto the island resort.

Hilton Head's developers had wisely kept it from becoming too commercial. Each building met rigid standards for blending into the environment. The resort was a harmonic combination of seascape with the Old South. Sugar beeches stretched out from thick forests of pine, moss-laden live oak, and crape myrtle.

"It's lovely," Allison said excitedly, having edged away from Spencer to gaze out the passenger window. "I can't believe I've never come here before. Do you dock your yacht here all the time?"

"Depends. If business brings me to this part of the country, I prefer this port."

"Exactly what business are you in?"

"I emptied the refrigerator before I left," he said, wheeling into a supermarket parking lot. "We'd better stop for groceries."

Miffed because he had ignored her question, she stubbornly stayed in the car even when he came around and opened her door.

"Why is your business such a secret? Is it illegal?"

"No."

"What do you do, then?"

"I deal in a product."

"What product?"

"None of your business."

"What do you do with this product? Manufacture it? Market it? What?"

"I take it out of one country and transport it to another," he replied enigmatically.

She paled. "Smuggling? You're a smuggler?"

"Are you going to help me buy groceries or take potluck?" he demanded with mock sternness. With visions of black-market diamonds, drugs, and nuclear weapons in her head, she got out of the car.

As promised, they arrived at the yacht basin just as the sun was sinking into Calibogue Sound off the western point of the island. It was an awesome sight. The giant orange ball reflected a sheet of gold over the water and stained the sky with vermilion and violet.

"Didn't I tell you the sunset was spectacular?" Spencer whispered in her ear as they stood on the pier, his arm looped over her shoulder.

"Yes, but it's more than I expected."

Silent and rapt, they enjoyed the view until the sun had disappeared completely and day gave way to indigo twilight. "Come on, I'm ready for you to see the *Double Dealer*."

"That's the name of your boat?"

"None other."

"Does the name have significance?"

"None you want to know about."

"That's what I was afraid of."

He only laughed and called out "Ahoy there," as they reached their destination.

A young man about sixteen poked his head around a deck chair. "Hi, Mr. Raft. I didn't think you were due in today."

"I came back a few days early. Everything okay?" he asked the boy as he helped Allison onto the deck of the yacht.

"Shipshape. Hi," he said to Allison.

"Hello," she answered demurely. This young man was bound to know why she was here and it made her distinctly uncomfortable.

Spencer introduced him as belonging to the family who owned the boat docked next to his. "I hired Gary to keep an eye on things while I was away."

"We can settle up later," the young man said. "See ya." He jumped from the deck onto the pier and headed toward his family's boat.

"Tell your folks thanks for lending you to me."

"Sure."

With a wave he was gone, and they were left alone in the gathering darkness. "Let me show you around."

The yacht was sixty-two feet of comfort and luxury. Allison knew nothing about boats, but the *Double Dealer* seemed to have all the comforts of home compactly arranged. The decks were spotless. There wasn't one chip to be found anywhere in the white paint. The wood was highly varnished. The brass instruments sparkled.

The wheelhouse was equipped with every conceivable navigational device and looked more complex than the instrument panel on a 747. The galley was as modern as any kitchen. Three sides of the "den" were lined with a white leather sofa. It was carpeted in Mediterranean blue. There were stereo components, a videotape machine, a television, a wet bar. The one sleeping cabin was huge and extravagantly furnished with white suede chairs, black lacquered chests, and a full-sized bed tucked under a bank of windows at the prow. The adjoining head lacked a bathtub, but the shower and other appointments more than made up for that.

"You like?" he asked close to her ear as she gazed at the bedroom. It resembled an Oriental pleasure palace.

"I like," she said hoarsely. Then, rousing herself, she turned to him with a bright, nervous smile. "Very much."

"Good. Make yourself comfortable. It'll take me several trips to unload the car."

"Need any help?"

He kissed her quickly, but soundly. "No. You'd better get all the rest you can. You'll need it later."

With that suggestive warning and a swat on her fanny, he left. He carried the sacks of groceries from the car first, so the perishables could be refrigerated. She unloaded them and put them away as he went back for their suitcases.

When he deposited hers in the bedroom, he brushed his lips across hers. "One more trip."

She was stowing her things in the empty drawers he had told her to use when he returned carrying two glasses of chilled white wine.

"I thought we should get things off to a good start with a toast."

Taking the wine he offered her, she laughed. "I remember the last toast we made. I could barely see my glass. I couldn't see you at all."

"When you did get your first clear glimpse of me, were you disappointed?"

"Fishing for a compliment?"

"Yes."

Her smile gradually faded as she seriously studied the

features made rugged by hours of exposure to the elements. His eyes were mysteries that never failed to intrigue her, hooded by the untamed brows and framed by sunbursts of laugh lines. Their depth of color was breathtaking, but it was the vitality that one saw in them that was so arresting. They bespoke the vibrant personality of the man.

Around his well-shaped head, his hair lay in rakish disarray, lifted and tossed about by the sea breeze. His shirt was open halfway down his chest. That dense network of dark curly hair blanketed the tanned skin and curved muscles.

"No, I wasn't disappointed," she vowed softly.

A fleeting grin lifted the corners of his lips, then he clinked his glass to hers. "To us. And the success of this trip."

She sipped, staring at him over the rim of her glass. After only one swallow of the cold, crisp wine, he took the glass from her and, along with his, set it aside.

He curved his hand round the back of her neck under her hair. "I've been hungry for you all day." He drew her closer to him inch by slow inch. "I can't wait any longer."

His neck bent and his lips found hers open and waiting for his kiss. As his thumb gently stroked the underside of her jaw, his tongue lazily explored her mouth. It swirled magically, probed symbolically, eliciting delicious reactions in every part of her body and soft moans from her throat.

He pulled back slightly to sip at her lips. Then his tongue plundered again with a mounting savagery that excited her. His arms closed around her like bands of steel. He hugged her to him, fitting their bodies together like pieces of a puzzle, nestling his masculinity in the cove of her femininity. His hands slid to her derrière, pressed, lifted, massaged.

Then his hands settled on either side of her hips. With slowly revolving thumbs, he investigated the smoothness of her hipbones. At his touch, the lower part of her abdomen was suffused with warmth, a warmth that spread through her like spilled honey.

"Spencer," she gasped softly.

A heartbeat later, he had rid her of her belt and was lowering her to the bed. He tore open his shirt. She got only a passing glimpse of his magnificent chest before he lowered himself over her for a searing kiss that required all her attention.

He slipped a hand beneath her top and, with tantalizing leisure, tiptoed his fingers up her ribs to the undercurve of her breast. Her back arched off the bed and she called his name with a plaintive moan. Only then did his hand cover her. He moved it in ever-declining circles until he felt the peak hardening in the center of his palm, then his fingertips closed around the tiny bud and plucked it into tighter arousal.

"Oh my God," Allison groaned as the rough tips of his fingers fanned her.

He sat up and, catching the hem of the top, raised it over her breasts. He caught his breath, held it, and only let it out as he said, "You're beautiful."

Guiding her arms above her head, he peeled the top off and heedlessly flung it aside. He captured her wrists in one loose fist and kept them there far behind her head so his view would be unrestricted.

Her breasts were full and round, crowned with a delicate shade of rose. The areolas were puckered from his caress. Their sweet centers strained upward as though beseeching his touch. They trembled with need.

"I've wanted to taste you for so long."

He lowered his head over her. Allison, disbelieving this was happening to her, tucked her chin against her chest and raised her head in time to see his lips closing around her nipple. The first touch of his tongue was like an electric shock that zephyred through her. With a sharp cry, her head fell back on the bed and she clamped her teeth tight over her lower lip to keep from crying out again. Her hips rose and fell restlessly as his mouth worked its magic.

Once again she raised her head and watched as his tongue danced around the tautened peaks of her breasts in turn. Darting quickly, curling languidly, licking vigorously. Until she was shiny and wet. Then lifting away the moisture with tenderly nibbling lips.

"Darling," he whispered when he chanced to catch her watching him. "You are wonderful." He covered her again, pressing his bare chest against hers. His lips were hot, his tongue salacious in its violation of her mouth.

He rolled them to their sides and wedged one of his knees between hers. He kissed her repeatedly, rampantly, until they were breathless. Lifting one of her hands from his shoulder, he laid it against his heart. The hairs were silky beneath her palm. What a joy it was to trap each thudding beat of his heart in her hand.

"My heart is pounding," he rasped. "See what you do to me here." Then he carried her hand down past his waist to the fly of his pants. He fashioned her hand into a shallow cup and filled it with his bulging hardness. "And here."

Suddenly it wasn't desire that filled her veins, it was panic. Panic just as passionately felt as the previous desire. Coldly it rushed through her, filled her throat with its brassy taste.

He was huge, and hard, and so dangerously, terrifyingly male that she yanked her hand from him and pushed herself away. Rolling to the far side of the bed, she sat up and braced herself on its edge in a vain attempt to regain her equilibrium. Reaching for her discarded blouse, she covered her front.

For long, still moments only their harsh breathing filled the dark room. Neither moved. Allison kept her head bowed, her eyes pinched shut.

At last he said, "Allison, do you care to tell me what's wrong?"

Wrong, wrong, wrong, the word tolled in her head. Every time a woman said no, it was assumed something was wrong with her. Well, in this instance, wasn't there?

"I tried to tell you I was no good at this sort of thing," she flared, still keeping her back to him. It was uncovered, naked, vulnerable to his eyes which she knew were piercing straight through her. "You wouldn't listen."

"I thought you were very good at this," he remarked with a coolness that, rather than alleviating her distress, only increased it. "Was I going too fast? Did I offend you?"

"I don't want to talk about it."

"Well, dammit, I do!" he shouted.

Over her shoulder she shot him a poisonous look. "If

your ego is bruised, rest assured. It wasn't because of you that I stopped, it was because of me."

"What about you? You didn't want to touch me?"

She swallowed. "No."

After a short silence, he said, "I see. Can you tell me why?"

"No."

"Do I repulse you?"

Terrify, yes. Repulse, no. "No."

"Surely my arousal was obvious. It couldn't have shocked you to touch me."

"It did!" The words were out before she could call them back.

"I don't understand. You know what a sexually aroused man feels like."

She came off the bed like a shot and spun around to face him. "In theory I know. I know all about the mechanics. It's the application I know nothing about."

There! It was out! She saw his stunned face only a second before she turned around again and shoved her arms into the sleeves of her top and pulled it on.

She heard him shift on the bed. "You're a *virgin*?"

"You needn't make it sound like a disease. I promise it's not a contagious condition." She went to the windows and breathed deeply of the cool sea air, trying to clear her head. Why hadn't she stayed in her lab where she was in control? Why had she ventured into something she had no experience with, where she was bound to make a fool of herself?

She kept her eyes glued to the horizon. Spencer got off the bed and came to stand close behind her. When he laid his hands on her shoulders, she jerked in reaction.

"Hey, hey, no more of that. I told you once I wouldn't force my attentions on you." He spoke softly, like a parent soothing a frightened child. He turned her around to face him, though he was kind enough to press her face into the curve of his throat and not force her to meet his eyes.

"I'm sorry, Allison. I swear I am. It never occurred to me that you were a virgin. I've approached this whole thing with the assumption that you had been with a man." His fingers threaded through her hair and she thought she felt a tender kiss being planted on the top of her head. "Poor baby. I came on like gangbusters. No wonder you flinched away from familiarities. From now on, we'll take things slow and easy. On your timetable, okay?"

Her nose was nestled in the furry warmth of his chest. Her head was filled with the scent of his skin. His taste was still lingering on her lips. She was being seduced by his considerate tenderness now as much as she had been seduced by his wild passion only moments ago.

Bravely she raised her head to meet his blue gaze. "I'll understand if you want to send me back to Atlanta."

His eyes wandered over her tangled wreath of red hair, her limpid green eyes, her mouth that was still swollen from their kisses. "Not a chance, lady," he whispered. "You're staying right here with me." He wanted to kiss her badly, but instead drew a deep breath and stepped back. "I don't think either of us feels like cooking tonight. Why don't we go out for dinner?"

His sensitivity touched her. Staying on the boat alone might make for more awkwardness. They needed people, lights, diverting activity. "That sounds wonderful. I'd like to shower and change."

"Sure. You take the bathroom first. I'll wait up on deck until you're finished."

As soon as she was showered, she wrapped herself in a terry-cloth robe and went to the stairs to call him. He took them two at a time on his way down, ducking his head to clear the door.

He stopped on the bottom step when he saw her in the thigh-length robe. "I'll dress out here while you're in the bathroom," she said quickly.

"Fine." His voice sounded like a dull blade being scraped over a whetstone.

She donned one of her new dresses, a spaghetti-strap T-shirt dress with a dropped waist from which a gathered skirt fell to the middle of her calf. It was a color she had never worn before, a bright fuchsia pink. Ann had insisted that with the right lip and cheek color she could handle it. When she studied her image in the mirror, the color of the dress was the least of her worries.

Nor did Spencer notice the color when he joined her on deck fifteen minutes later. His hair was still damp from his shower and he smelled of soap and cologne. But she glanced at him worriedly, unconsciously twisting her hands in front of her.

As though equipped with radar, his eyes dropped right to where Allison knew they would.

The dress was like a dance leotard with a skirt sewed on to it. It was designed to fit like a second skin and it did. Which was the problem. "Ann unpacked all my bras. Probably while I was answering the door to let you in this morning."

With a supreme effort, he dragged his eyes from her breasts and reached out to take her arm. As he helped her on to the pier, he whispered querulously, "I only hope you don't get cold tonight."

"Cold?"

"Yeah. If your nipples become any more pronounced than they already are, all my good intentions to take it slow and easy are going to be shot to hell."

CHAPTER EIGHT

He was a perfect gentleman all through dinner, though Allison knew it was taxing him to be. She would never have thought a man of Spencer's sophistication could get rattled, but he was edgy and nervous, his eyes often scuttling over her breasts, a pained expression on his face. Allison would have felt sorry for him were it not for the feminine pride it gave her to know that she was responsible for his distress.

"I see you're not allergic to shellfish," he remarked as she polished off a plate of succulent shrimp scampi.

She laughed. "No. And I don't particularly like red meat, so you can imagine how I felt about eating that virtually raw prime rib that night. Much less the pâté." She shivered.

"That's why I liked you right away. You took it on the chin all evening and rallied every time." He reached for her hand across the candlelit table. "The only thing I couldn't figure out was why you were going to such great lengths to please a fiancé you didn't love. At least it was obvious to me you didn't love Davis."

"You're a very intuitive man."

"I think so. And if you knew all the intuitions I've had about you, you'd be blushing."

Even without knowing them, she blushed.

Hand in hand they strolled through Harbor Town, which was the hub of activity on the island once the sun went down. Restaurants and fabulous boutiques formed a credit card–splurging maze. Children and senior citizens, families and lovers, ate and drank and sang and danced in the balmy night air.

Spencer found them seats on the low stone wall bordering the pier. They enjoyed the show being presented on the stage beneath the sprawling live-oak tree, Liberty Oak, which the harbor had been built around. The young singer's voice was clear, his gaiety infectious. They clapped their hands in time to the music and laughed at his familiar vaudevillian jokes.

Spencer sat close, his attention on Allison as much as on the show. When the performance concluded, they were swallowed by the crowd. In order not to lose Allison in the throng, he moved her in front of him and placed a hand on each side of her waist.

His fingers were strong against her ribs. His palms seemed to have matched themselves to the curve of her waist. The sundress was deeply scooped out in the back and she could feel the gauzy cloth of his shirt against her skin. At a bottleneck in the progression of the crowd, she was pressed close against him. Her spine made contact with his chest, as the first three buttons of his shirt had been left undone.

Thankfully he couldn't see her face, for she closed her eyes and luxuriated in the accidental caress. He wasn't impervious to it. His hands flexed tighter around her waist and she felt his lips moving in her hair. As though both were thinking about it so intensely, it happened— her bottom came to rest snugly against the fly of his trousers.

When they were finally on their way again, both were breathing raggedly, but trying vainly to appear unaffected. Once they reached the deck of the *Double Dealer*, Allison became shy and awkward again.

"Would you like some wine?" he asked.

She had drunk two glasses with dinner with no ill effects. "No. I've had my limit." She smiled apologetically. "I'm not much good at anything, even drinking."

He hitched his hands on his hips and assumed an angry stance. "You're damn good at putting yourself down." Turning his back on her, he paced the deck to the prow, which was pointed oceanward, then back to where she was standing at the stern. "If I didn't want you here, you wouldn't be here, got that? Now, that's the last time I'm going to say it. Stop acting so meek and apologetic and tell me what you want to do for the rest of the evening. Watch TV or listen to some of my collector's records or play cards or what?"

His temper had piqued hers. Who did he think he was, shouting at her? "I want to go to bed," she said coldly. "It's been a long day."

She sashayed past him, her soft skirt swirling around

her bare legs. As she brushed by him on her way below, he caught her hand and spun her around. He pulled her against him hard and, catching her hair in one fist, gently yanked her head back.

The moon was reflected in the deep blue of his eyes. His face was shadowed. A slow, devilish grin spread over his mouth, making his teeth look startlingly white in his dark face.

"You're good at one thing—getting mad. You get madder faster than any woman I've ever known. You're like a match ready to catch fire at any moment. It must be the red hair," he mused, rubbing the thick strands between his fingers. "But I like it," he said in a low growl. "Your temper excites the hell out of me."

His eyes hungrily roamed over her face, taking in the haughty tilt of her chin, the green defiance in her eyes, the crackling life of her hair. They scaled down to enjoy the view of her breasts, which swelled out of the top of the dress because of the tight way he was holding her.

His whole body groaned with desire. But he remembered his promise. Looking as she did right now, if he kissed her, he wouldn't be able to stop until he was buried deep inside her. Then she would no longer trust him. He had to win her trust before he could win her body.

Gently he set her away from him. He saw something flicker in her eyes and hoped that it might be disappointment. "If you need anything you can't find, call me. I'll be out here on deck for a while. Good night, Allison."

"Good night." At the entrance to the cabin, she turned. He hadn't moved, but was still looking after her. She wet her lips, ashamed of her earlier attitude. "I had a good time tonight, Spencer. Thank you."

His smile was quick and abrupt, as was the acknowledging nod of his head. She went below to the bedroom, which was far more opulent than it had a right to be. When she pulled back the bedspread, she was amazed to find white satin sheets beneath. She'd never slept on anything but percale. She put on one of the pajamas Ann had pressed her to buy. It was a two-piece black silk. The top was cut in a deep V in front and held up by two thin straps. The bikini bottom was so skimpy, she wondered why she had even bothered with it.

The combination of the silk, her own naked skin, and the embracing satin sheets was a sensual experience she never could have imagined. She felt the way Rasputin must every time she approached him with her fur glove. She virtually purred as she stretched languidly, wallowing in the sensations that seemed to touch every part of her being.

When she heard Spencer coming below to use the bathroom, she rolled to her side, giving him her back, and pretended to be asleep. She heard the toilet flush, heard water splashing, heard him switching off the light before he opened the door and came out. She lay perfectly still.

It was only when she heard the whisper of his shirt being removed, the rasp of his zipper, the thud of his shoes on the floor that her eyes popped open. And when the other side of the bed dipped to his weight, she turned over and sat upright.

"What are you doing?"

He paused in the act of pulling the top sheet over him. Moonlight came in through the windows, bathing the whole room with silver light and making his body something out of an erotic dream. Against his darkly tanned skin, the white, alarmingly brief underwear only drew attention to his generous masculinity. His body hair was a sexual stimulant in itself. Dense and curly here, fine and silky there, a mere dusting elsewhere. A woman could spend hours studying each texture, each thrilling pattern.

"I'm getting into bed," he answered calmly.

She was so distraught by this turn of events that she forgot the plunging V of the pajama top and the way her unhampered breasts swayed beneath the clinging silk. Only when Spencer's hooded eyes dropped to that region did she catch up a corner of the sheet and cover herself. "You can't sleep here."

"Watch me." He pushed his long legs between the sheets and laid his head on the pillow, sighing contentedly. Linking his fingers, he turned them outward and stretched like a lazy panther. Then he folded his hands behind his head, arched his back off the mattress and yawned broadly. Only when he relaxed again did he look at her, cocking an eyebrow and asking in all innocence, "Do you intend to sleep sitting up?"

His body moved like a well-oiled machine. Allison found herself tongue-tied and entranced by the play of muscle, the tone of skin, the grace of coordination. When she could speak, she forced emphasis into her voice.

"I don't intend to sleep at all, at least not here." She slung off the sheet as though escaping the clutches of something seductive and decadent just in the nick of time. Thrashing bare legs to free herself, she rolled to the side of the bed and sat up on its edge. Her feet hit the floor and she started to stand.

"Oh yes, you are." He grabbed for a handhold and what he caught was the elastic band of her pajama bottom. His fingers curled down inside it and formed a tight fist around a handful of black silk.

She froze, for to move would mean leaving her panty in his grip and her bottom . . .

"Let go," she said breathlessly.

He began to laugh. It started as a low rumble in his chest until it built into a full-fledged booming laugh. "Not until hell freezes over, honey. But you can leave anytime you want. Go on, move. I dare you."

"You're horrible!"

"Now, now, no name calling." He gave the panty a playful jerk and she gasped. "Um, very nice. Round, smooth, soft. If you don't want me to go all the way with it, you'd better get that sweet little tush back in this bed."

Gradually, eating crow and swallowing pride every inch of the way, she lowered her bottom back onto the bed. He released the panty, but she didn't have time to leap away before his arm curled around her rib cage. He hauled her to his side of the bed, where she landed against him with a plop. The pajama top became twisted in the tussle and her bare stomach was cushioned by his hair-whorled one. He anchored her above him with an arm across her back. She braced her arms stiffly on either side of his shoulders and glared down into his satanically triumphant face.

"The view from here isn't bad either," he mused, unabashedly staring down into the gaping pajama top at her breasts.

She struggled to release herself. "You're a pervert, a sex fiend, a—"

"Your temper is going to get you in a helluva lot of trouble one of these days, Red," he chided softly, clicking his tongue.

"Let me get up."

He grinned the smile of a hedonistic despot. "I'm the one who's getting up. And unless you're prepared to remedy the consequences of that, you'd better stop squirming." Immediately she ceased all movement. Her eyes were wide and frightened as she stared down at him. "Now are you ready to listen to what I want to say, what I would have explained if you hadn't flown off the handle?"

"Yes," she said huskily. He wasn't bluffing. She could feel the pressure of his manhood against her belly. Her body wasn't immune to their position either. Bare skin against bare skin must certainly be the ultimate human pleasure. She had the ridiculous desire to slide along his tall frame, touch his body with hers everywhere possible.

"All right, then." Slowly he relaxed his arm across her back and let her roll off him. Still, he kept his arms loosely around her as they lay facing each other. Judiciously she scooted her legs away from his, but he smiled. Her breathing was as unsteady as his. If he knew anything about women, and he knew plenty, she was just as aroused as he.

"This is the only bed on the boat," he began.

"You could sleep on one of the sofas."

"I could, but I'm disinclined to."

"Then I will."

"No, Allison." He cupped her cheek in his palm and lowered his voice to soft confidentiality. "We're here to accomplish a mission, aren't we?"

Her eyes couldn't seem to stay away from his bare chest. Under the guise of shyness, they treated themselves to a visual feast. "Yes. But under the circumstances I wouldn't hold you to that."

"I still want to make a baby. And the only way we're ever going to hope for success is to break down your inhibitions and fears."

"I don't know if we ever will."

"You leave that to me," he said, softly kissing her forehead. Gradually the tension was ebbing out of her. She was no longer straining away from him. Of course the points of her breasts were touching his chest and driving him into a fine madness. He could feel her fragrant breath filtering through his chest hair. But he corralled his passions. "The first thing you must get used to is having a man in bed with you, get used to the feel of his body against yours. Granted?"

She swallowed. "I suppose so."

"Okay, then. Give me a good-night kiss and we'll go to sleep."

She pecked him lightly on the lips. "Good night."

"Allison," he said drolly as she turned to the other side.

"Hm?"

"Do you call that a kiss? Is that the way I kiss you?"

She faced him again, pressing her hot cheek into the pillow. "No."

"Kiss me the way I'd kiss you. You've done it many times."

"I know, but those times were different."

"Why?"

"Because I was merely responding to you, not initiating it."

"You don't think men want to be made love to every once in a while instead of the other way around?"

"Do they?"

"I do." He took her hand and laid it over his heart. He lightly scratched the back of her hand. "Kiss me, Allison."

She looked into his face. His eyebrows cast his eyes into deep shadows, but they still glowed like sapphires. She loved the shape of his nose and the way his nostrils flared slightly over that sensual mouth. The firm determination of his jaw and chin had always appealed to her. It specified a man of character. The lines radiating from his eyes testified that he was full of wit and charm.

She studied him for long moments, thinking only how much his weather-etched face appealed to her, how much she liked the roguish dishevelment of his dark hair, how much she loved the man, even his arrogance and highhandedness. That made it easy for her to lean forward and press her mouth to his.

He lay docile and motionless. His lips remained closed. At first she only pressed her mouth more firmly against his. But this wasn't the way he had kissed her, not even at the first kiss.

Daringly she touched his lips with her tongue, then quickly withdrew it.

"Yes, Allison, yes," he moaned, lifting one of his hands to her back and spreading his fingers wide over it.

When she pressed her tongue forward again, his lips were parted and it slid into the wet heat of his mouth. She uttered a small groan when the tip of her tongue touched his. Without having to think about it or weighing the wisdom of it, she inched up and over him, higher and closer, as her head bent over his. Her hair formed a curtain on either side of their faces. His free hand buried itself in the silky strands.

She raised her hands and tunneled all ten fingers into his hair, holding his head fast as her mouth unleashed its hunger. Her tongue pumped against his and he responded. They thrust and parried with each other. The kiss became more ardent with each passing second until they whirled in a maelstrom of passion.

Her thighs slid open to straddle his. When he sent his tongue burrowing deep into her mouth, she reflexively rolled her hips forward.

Blasting the walls with a vicious curse, Spencer pushed her away and sat up in the same panicked manner she had when he'd gotten into the bed. Raising his knees, he propped his elbows on them and dropped his head into his hands. His rib cage was like a bellows as his breath heaved in and out.

Allison cowered against the pillows, her respiration none too steady. How long had they been kissing? Minutes? Hours? Time, space, nothing had relevance except the taste of his mouth and the feel of his hands and the warm strength of his body beckoning to hers. A responsive cord had been struck and she had hovered on the brink of losing control.

At last Spencer sighed and flopped onto his back. He gazed up at her, a tender gaze, and tucked a strand of hair behind her ear.

"Didn't I do it right?"

He smiled sadly. "You did it perfectly. Too perfectly. Understand?"

When enlightenment dawned, she quickly lay down beside him, but kept her distance. "Yes, I think so."

He picked her hand off the sheet and brought it to his mouth for a sweet kiss. "Good night, love."

"Good night."

He turned to the far side of the bed, facing away from her. They didn't speak or move again, but Allison didn't think he fell asleep any faster than she did.

She awoke to the gentle rocking motion of the boat and the throbbing vibration of its powerful engine. Prying her eyes open, she rolled to her side. She was alone in the bed. The sun was still new and hazy.

Getting out of bed and padding to the windows she could see the coastline shrinking in the distance. She pulled on a robe, and after a quick trip to the bathroom, ventured onto the deck. Spencer was at the wheel, staring out over the Atlantic as the prow of the boat neatly cleaved the water. His back was to her and she didn't disturb him.

On a sudden inspiration, she went into the tiny galley. A pot of coffee had already been perked. It was too strong for her liking, but a dollop of the cream they'd bought yesterday made it drinkable. There was no other evidence of breakfast having been started. She set about the task.

While the bacon was frying, she ducked back into the bedroom and pulled on a pair of shorts and a top.

Gathering her hair into a ponytail, she tied a bright scarf around it. On bare feet she raced back to the galley in time to keep the bacon from burning.

Fifteen minutes later, she called up to the wheelhouse. "Has the captain of this tub had his breakfast yet?"

Spencer turned around, his eyes lighting up at the sight of her in a way that made her heart flip-flop. "No, matey."

"Does he want some?"

In answer, he cut the motor and followed her down into the galley. The table was set and crowded with serving platters of fluffy scrambled eggs, crisp bacon, toasted English muffins, jams and jellies, and sliced honeydew melon.

"Is this for me?"

"Are you the captain?"

"Aye, aye."

"Then it's for you."

The captain helped his first mate into her chair before he dug into the breakfast with enthusiastic appreciation.

"This is great. Really. Why didn't you tell me you could cook?"

"You didn't ask."

"I didn't care."

"You didn't ask if I could make love either."

His head snapped up and he pushed down a swallow before he said, "I didn't care." He reached across the table and took her hand. "In fact, in a very old-fashioned way, I'm glad you haven't been with another man. I have the honor of being first."

The moment was rife with emotion. He was actually saying that he found her awkwardness and inexperience endearing. Another reason to fall in love with him. They were mounting up at an alarming rate.

"Where are we going?" she asked. Actually she didn't give a fig about their destination as long as she could stay with him.

"Just out cruising for a few hours. I wanted to show off my navigational skills."

"Can I drive it?"

"Pilot it," he corrected.

"Pilot it. Can I?"

"You have to wash the dishes first."

"Okay," she said, standing to carry their dishes to the sink. "But you have to make the bed."

"That's mutiny."

"That's fair."

"Deal," he conceded. To seal the bargain, he affectionately slapped her fanny.

They saw only a few other vessels and those from a distance. He made her sit on his lap as she handled the wheel. It was a heady feeling to guide such a large boat, but nothing compared to the thrills she felt when Spencer laid his hands on the tops of her bare thighs and nibbled at her shoulder.

"Don't run into anything bigger than us," he cautioned.

"I'm not used to this." She didn't know if she was speaking of his caresses or steering the boat. "You'd better help me."

He wrapped his arms around her from behind, lacing his fingers over her stomach and resting his chin on her shoulder. "You're doing fine. Just take her nice and easy," he whispered as his thumbs traced the lower curve of her breast. Moved up. Caressed more boldly. "She'll respond to the lightest touch." When his thumbs swept over the crests of her breasts, he was proven correct.

"Are you talking about the boat?" Allison asked on a short breath.

"Of course," he assured her, but let his hands sift down her ribs onto more neutral territory.

When she'd had her fill of piloting, he turned the motor off. "It's a calm sea and a beautiful day. Why don't we drop anchor and laze away the rest of the afternoon?"

"Sounds wonderful." She'd never been on an ocean-going vessel in her life, yet the vastness of the Atlantic didn't faze her. She felt perfectly safe on the *Double Dealer* and wondered where this newfound intrepidness came from. It must be a by-product of the love that had started as a fine trickle and had now developed into a gushing wellspring inside her.

She slipped into one of her new bikinis while Spencer loaded a tray with cold cuts and cheese, a loaf of French bread, sliced cantaloupe, fresh strawberries, and a box of cookies. He carried an ice chest with soft drinks and beer up on deck so they wouldn't have to make so many trips below.

He almost dropped the heavy chest on his big toe when he came up on deck to find Allison stretched out in one of the lounge chairs spreading on suntanning gel. The bronze-colored bikini barely qualified as such. It was a mere four scraps of fabric held together by a series of strings.

Even through the large sunglasses she wore, he could see her self-consciousness as she glanced up at him and caught his ravenous expression. "Ann made me buy it."

"Remind me to thank her," he said thickly, staring at the triangles that weren't doing a very good job of containing her breasts. The beguiling delta between her thighs captured his attention and he couldn't seem to tear his eyes away.

"Spencer, stop it!" she cried, crossing her arms over her chest. "If you don't stop looking at me like you're about to devour me, I'll go change. You make me extremely uncomfortable."

His eyebrows bobbed up and down Groucho-style and he waved an imaginary cigar. "If you think you're uncomfortable—"

"May I have a cold drink, please," she asked primly.

Laughing, he opened the chest and delved into the crushed ice to fish out a can for her. He popped the top off and extended it toward her, but held it just out of her reach. She had to lean over to take it and when she did her breasts spilled around the small cups of the bikini. "Thank you," she said with asperity, snatching the can from his hand.

"Thank *you*."

She shot him a venomous look as she lay back in a more modest position. But her huffiness turned to fascination as he stood and peeled off his shirt. She had almost gotten used to his bare legs . . . almost. He'd been wearing swim trunks under the shirt all morning. But the sight of him in nothing more than that well-fitting pair of navy blue trunks was breathtaking. Just as she had always imagined, he was sleek and leanly muscled. The skin on his upper arms stretched smoothly over sculpted curves her hands longed to caress.

His chest was wide, with flat, dark nipples sheltered

in the mat of hair. Between the corrugated rib cage, his stomach was hard and taut. His abdomen tapered into narrow hips. He had tight buns, firm thighs, and the calves of a runner.

"Want some lunch?" he asked as he dropped down onto the chaise beside hers.

To give her mouth something else to do besides gape and salivate, she said, "Sure. This all looks so good."

As they ate, she questioned him about the time he spent on the boat. "Don't you ever get lonesome?"

"Yes." He had finished eating and was trailing a lazy finger up and down the inside of her arm as it rested on the chaise. "I told you that I'd become tired of chasing all over the world."

He could have been stroking her tummy in that same indolent manner, for that's where she felt the feathery sensations. "Have you ever been frightened out in the middle of the ocean? During a storm, for instance."

"A few times. I'm extremely cautious and try to avoid bad weather. My business isn't so pressing that I can't delay meetings for a few days if need be."

"What kind of meetings?"

"You have beautiful breasts."

"You're changing the subject."

"Uh-uh. You're changing the subject. My mind has been on your breasts for days."

She was too relaxed and happy to protest. She yawned, stretching expansively. "I'm full and sleepy. I think I'll turn over and drowse. What are you going to do?"

"Lie here and watch you drowse."

She rolled to her stomach and laid her cheek on her

folded hands. "Um, the sun feels so good and—what are you doing?"

"Untying your bikini."

"I know that. Why?"

"So you won't have any unsightly marks. We can't let that happen, can we? Not that anything on this back could be unsightly." He planted a kiss on her shoulder. "Besides, I need to put some of this stuff on your back or you'll burn. Now be quiet and go to sleep."

"Aye, aye, captain," she said around another yawn. His hands did feel marvelous as they smoothed the gel over her skin. He knew just the places to touch, exactly the right amount of pressure to apply. Her whole body hummed with pleasure as his thumbs dug into the small of her back and rotated slowly. She drifted to sleep with his fingers feeling their way up and down her spine.

Spencer lay back on his chaise and studied the woman lying beside him. In the bright sunlight her hair was dazzling. It had been piled on top of her head, not in the prim bun she wore to the lab, but in a loose knot that trailed coy tendrils over her neck and shoulders. He thought that mussed, tumbled look was significant. It indicated her careless disregard for the usual rigidity of her life. It gave him hope.

Her skin was the color of ripe apricots, smooth and slick now with the gel he'd applied. He couldn't help but imagine his hands examining its texture, his mouth sampling luscious spots.

In profile, her back defined suppleness. It dipped at her waist and rose at her hips. In that shallow valley between there was a cluster of white peach fuzz that spun around twin dimples. Her thighs were long and slender, her calves gentle mounds he knew would fit his palms perfectly. He longed to press his mouth to the arch of her foot and kiss each of the ten toes.

A strange and wonderful glow spread around his heart. He wanted her, yes. In a most carnal way, yes. But he wanted her in every other way too. He wanted her spirit and that short, fierce temper, her intelligence, her insecurities, her innocence. He wanted to teach her every way there was to make love and wanted her to teach him every mysterious thing about her that made her unique.

Was he in love with her, then?

He thought he must be. For days he had known that once he made love to her, it wouldn't be an ending, but a beginning. Was that love? Was that the nature of that entity that had eluded him all his adult life? Until now. Until this ache had seized him and wouldn't let him go. And the hell of it was, he didn't want to be let go.

Under her raised arm he could see the curve of her breast. He longed to touch it, longed to slide his hand beneath it and let it fill his palm. He wanted to have its peak harden between his caressing fingers again, to kiss it, suck it, listen to the low mating sounds that gurgled in her throat when his tongue nudged it.

God! He was dying. It was almost painful to stand up, but he struggled to his feet. In a storage closet, he rummaged for the ladder that hooked over the side of the yacht. He locked it into place. Then with one last look at the woman who now dominated his mind and controlled his body, he dived over the side.

CHAPTER NINE

Later, she couldn't say what woke her up, nor why she had awakened with her heart in her throat and her blood pounding. She suddenly sat up on the chaise. Unheeded, her bikini top slid to the deck.

Spencer was no longer lying in the chaise beside her. "Spencer?" She blinked against the blinding sunlight. She stood up and turned three hundred and sixty degrees, her eyes combing the yacht for sight of him. "Spencer?" she called more loudly.

She ran to the other side of the boat, calling his name in mounting panic. Where was he? She checked the wheelhouse and the galley, the den and the bedroom. He wasn't on the boat!

"Spencer!" she cried as she emerged from below, frantically swinging her head from side to side. "Spencer!"

"Here, Allison."

Her heart was thudding, but she heard his voice over

the racket in her ears. "Spencer," she whispered in vast relief, before shouting, "Where?"

"On the starboard side. Is something wrong?"

She raced to the right side of the yacht, but didn't see him. Then he repeated her name, his own voice now laced with concern.

"Allison, are you all right?"

She followed the sound of his voice and for the first time noticed the ladder hooked to the side of the craft. Running to the rail, she looked down to see him climbing up the rungs, dripping sea water.

"You were swimming!" she exclaimed in agitation. *"Swimming?"*

"What did you think I was doing? Is something wrong?"

By now he was swinging one long leg over the rail and stepping onto the deck.

"Wrong? You scared me half to death. I woke up and didn't know where you were. I was all alone out here in the middle of the Atlantic Ocean and I don't know how to drive this damn boat or even how to start it. And for godsakes there are sharks and God knows what else in that water. And—"

Her face crumpled and she began to cry. His arms, cool and wet, went around her and drew her to him. He cupped the back of her head and pressed her face against his throat. Her arms clung to his waist.

"I'm sorry I scared you. I go overboard all the time. I didn't think to mention it. I was never more than twenty feet away from the boat. Are you better now?"

His hand was gentle as he tilted her head up. Water dripped from his hair and fell like rain onto her face. "I feel like an idiot. I don't know why I panicked. I just felt so lost and"—she was momentarily stunned by the loving intent in his eyes and the earnestness of his expression as he looked down into her face—"lost and alone without you," she finished in a whisper.

Simultaneously they realized that they were locked in an embrace, bare chest to bare breasts, bare thighs meshed. Droplets of water clung to his chest hair before falling to run in crystal rivulets down the curves of her breasts. She was standing with her feet close together; his were planted on either side of them. Tummies breathed in unison. Maleness and femininity were complementing each other.

For hours her skin had been soaking up the sun. His had just been cooled by ocean water. Now the heat came seeping out of hers to warm his. The contrast was delicious.

Their eyes transmitted a thousand silent messages, communicating on a level that surpassed spoken language. They came together of one accord.

Their heads tilted in different directions as though on cue. She raised her arms to lock behind his bending neck as his arms encircled her waist. She went up on tiptoe as he urged her body closer to his.

When their lips met, their sighs of pleasure and pain mingled to create one hungry sound of reciprocated need. His lips were cold, but his tongue was hot as with one swift thrust it claimed her mouth. The kiss was long and deep, restraint-banishing and bone-melting.

She licked the salty taste off his lips. He groaned her name and pressed the small of her back, arching her against his body. His chest hair abraded her nipples like

silk bristles and she murmured his name when they pouted
with desire.

Spencer felt their distention against his chest and knew
what it meant. He put enough space between them to
cradle her face between his palms. He pierced her eyes
with his, asking the monumental question.

With trembling fingers she touched his mouth, then
his cheekbone, then his brows. Lowering her eyes, she
squeezed them shut and whispered, "Make love to me,
Spencer."

He wasted neither word nor motion in taking her
hand and leading her down the steps into the cabin. The
bedroom was cool and dim, with a breeze blowing in
through the windows.

"In here first," he said, leading her into the head.

"Why?"

He turned on the taps of the shower. "Because you're
slippery with suntan oil and when I reach for something,
I want to be able to grasp it." His teasing wink settled her
nerves. She even laughed, a throaty, sexy laugh that she
couldn't believe had come from her. "And I'm covered
with saltwater, which when it dries is going to itch and I
don't want to be distracted. Here, get in."

He stepped into the shower stall and pulled her in
with him. Only something as fluid as water could have
found its way between their bodies, so close did they
stand to each other. Spencer picked up a bar of soap and
handed it to her. "If you'll do the honors for me, I'll return the favor."

She lathered her hands, then laid them on either side
of his neck. She worked her way down slowly, sliding her

fingers over his shoulders, taking time to study the design of bone and muscle. She loved the hollow at the base of his throat. When she leaned forward to kiss it softly, he placed a finger beneath her chin, brought her mouth up to his, and kissed her with intimate thoroughness before she continued washing him.

Her hands glided over his chest, combing through the soapy hair, massaging the muscles. With uncharacteristic boldness, she smiled up at him as she curiously touched one of his nipples.

As it responded, he growled threateningly. "Just remember that turnabout is fair play."

That raspily spoken threat didn't deter the pads of her fingers from investigating him further, nor from coasting down his ribs and belly to play around his navel, hidden in its nest of hair.

"I'm going to take my trunks off now, Allison."

She jerked her hands back quickly. "All right."

Hooking his thumbs in either side of the waist, he peeled the trunks over his lower abdomen, his thighs, his legs, and stepped out of them.

She held her breath, hoping he wouldn't ask her to do something she wasn't yet prepared to do. But he merely held out his hand for the soap.

She passed him the fragrant bar. The foamy lather showed up white and lacy against his dark hands. He washed first her back. When it was done, he gently turned her again to face him. Her eyes slid shut against a wave of pleasure as his hands closed over her breasts.

"Feel good?" he asked.

"Yes."

"To me too."

He covered her front with soap, washing thoroughly, painstakingly, sensually. He even raised her arms and washed under them with sliding palms. His fingers trailed down the sides of her breasts, back up, down again, until her whole body was swaying with an erotic rhythm. He cupped the soft globes from beneath, lifted them and re-shaped them with a light squeezing motion. With his thumbs moving over the soap-slick tips, he brought her to a pinnacle of arousal.

She propped her arms on his shoulders and slumped forward. "I can't stand much more, Spencer."

"We've only just started, love."

He kissed her. The water continued its trickling jour-ney down their bodies as their mouths did what they wanted to do with their sexes—mate, unite, become one.

He slipped his hands under her bikini bottom and pressed his fingers into the lush curves of her derrière. "Is it all right?" He eased the garment down.

She nodded against his shoulder.

He pulled the bikini over her hips and down her thighs to past her knees. From there it slid to the shower floor. Allison and Spencer were left naked.

He embraced her tenderly. Holding only her upper arms in his hands, he inclined toward her. She gasped softly when she felt the hard maleness snuggling into her softness.

"I'm a man, Allison. That's all. You don't have to be afraid of me."

"I know."

He twisted around and turned off the taps. Allison stepped from the stall and quickly reached for a towel.

However, Spencer was right behind her and lifted it out of her hands. "I'm going to dry you."

The towel was fleecy and soft. His hands were those of an adoring servant. He blotted the water from her skin, moving from her shoulders and chest to her breasts, down her stomach to her thighs. Kneeling, he ran the towel down the length of her legs. Then he stood. "Turn around."

Her back was treated to the same loving care. He went to his knees again to dry the backs of her legs. When they were dry, he cast the towel aside and curled his hands around her hips. His fingers pressed into her abdomen. She covered them with her hands. She sucked her breath in sharply when his mouth opened over the small of her back and his tongue circled the dimples on either side of her spine.

"I wanted to taste that spot this afternoon," he said, coming to his feet. "It's a most intriguing spot."

"I've always been intrigued by your arms." She turned to face him.

He laughed. "My arms?"

Laying her hands on his biceps, she explained. "They're lean, but strong. The muscles are so well defined and the skin is tight. See the veins." Her fingertip tracked the distinct blue line. She kissed the hard muscle, then lightly closed her teeth around a bite. "It's like taking a bite out of an apple."

He hugged her to him. "Let's go to bed."

She went into the bedroom. He stayed in the bathroom only long enough to give himself a cursory once-over with the towel. She was lying between the satin sheets when he joined her. Her hair spilled over the pillow like liquid fire. Against the white sheets, her skin glowed richly with health and sun. Her eyes shone luminously green.

As he walked toward the bed, she kept her eyes resolutely high, not risking a glimpse at the lower part of his body. He lay down beside her. She had the sheet modestly draped over her breasts. He didn't bother with cover at all as he drew her into his embrace.

She came willingly, but he felt her timidity. He brushed back wayward strands of russet hair from her cheeks and kissed her lips lightly. "Tell me if I do anything that offends you or hurts you or that you don't like. Understand?"

"Yes."

He smiled that crooked, lazy grin that she loved. "Did you know that since I first danced with you, this is just where I wanted you, naked and lying in bed with me?"

"You're shameless. You told me the day you came to the lab that you wanted to get 'Ann' in your bed."

"And you sprayed coffee on me."

She laughed and buried her nose into the thatch of damply curling hair on his chest. "That should have been your first clue that something was amiss."

"Ah, Allison, you're gorgeous." He sighed, his eyes sliding over her face as he tipped her chin up.

"I'm a klutz."

"Not where kissing's concerned you're not."

She knew such pillow talk was only to flatter her, to put her at ease, to get her into a mellow mood conducive to lovemaking.

It was working. If she became any more mellow, the sheets were going to absorb her as she melted. "I'm a good kisser?" she asked, running her finger around the stubborn jut of his chin.

"Hm," he said, pecking her lips with his. He pressed his lips against her ear and whispered, "If we did nothing but kiss, I'd still get hard."

"You're already hard," she whispered back.

"That doesn't mean I'm going to give up the kissing step."

And with that, his lips opened over hers and he implanted his tongue in the receptive sweetness of her mouth. He inched closer. When his body came into intimate contact with hers, it confirmed what she already knew.

He was hard and warm and stirring. And rather than shrinking away from such blatant maleness, she gravitated toward it.

Their mouths played carnal games until the kisses weren't near enough. He peeled the sheet away and found her breasts warm and flushed and ready for his caresses.

His fingertips delighted in the satiny texture of her skin, in the fullness of her breasts, in the delicate coral peaks. His first touch elicited a soft moan from her lips. Her bare legs began to saw restlessly against his and her hips reached forward and upward.

"Let me taste you," he said as he dipped his head and took the milky tasting nipple between his lips. He suckled it gently.

Allison felt each precious tug deep in her womb and she knew then that she would become pregnant by this man. Her body couldn't flower so expectantly, yearn so deeply, react so drastically if it wasn't preparing itself for him. Her body would take his seed, take it and nurture it into a child. For her it would be a child born of love.

He moved to her other breast and his caresses were so light and deft, she had to open her eyes to make sure the delicious sensations weren't products of her own imagination. But there was his tongue finessing the rosy crests. Tasting, licking, sucking. She felt herself slipping toward an oblivion she both dreaded and craved.

"Spencer, please," she gasped, not sure of what she was begging him for. Fulfillment or release? Or were they the same?

He raised his head and turned it to gaze down her body, all of it. He wasn't going to be rushed. He was going to take his time, drink in every precious detail, every smooth curve and each alluring hollow.

"You're so beautiful, my love." He kissed the point where the sides of her rib cage met, then dragged his tongue down that shallow groove all the way to her navel.

Allison's breath rattled in her throat. "Oh, God." She sighed. She had never considered herself a sensual person. At his bidding, her body was oozing sensuality. One by one he was opening up tiny trapdoors and she felt herself sinking into a vat of consuming sexuality.

Her navel was virgin, too, but he deflowered it with his tongue. She caught handfuls of his hair, twisting the strands between her fingers as he continued to delve and discover.

He cupped the inside of her knee with his hand and lifted it, bending it. His palm caressed the underside of her thigh from knee to hip. Then he widened the space between her thighs and caressed the sensitive insides, his touch never becoming stronger than that of a butterfly's wing.

"Your skin is like silk. Warm silk." His breath disturbed the tangled curls on the V of her abdomen. Then he nuzzled that sweet nest as his fingers caressed between her thighs. He touched the soft womanly petals; he dipped into the dew gathered between them. "So sweet." She said his name in a low moan. "Does that hurt?" he asked, immediately stilling his caressing fingers.

"No, no, don't stop . . . you're inside me . . . Spencer . . . Spencer . . ."

"Shh, shh, you're wonderful. Do you hear me, Allison? You're beautiful." He eased himself between her thighs and replaced his fingers with his lips.

The world began to fall away beneath her. Tiny chips at first, then chunks of the sphere she knew slipped away. She reached out for a handhold and found his hair, thick and silky. She wound her fingers through it. The gentle laving of his agile tongue was relentless . . . until . . . until what was left of her splintered into fragments of dazzling light and scattered into a new universe.

When the last of the aftershocks had subsided and she opened her eyes, Spencer was lying above her, smiling down into her face with a tenderness that bordered on undiluted love. She opened her mouth to speak, but was seized by another series of blissful sensations.

Closing her eyes, she squeezed the walls of her body around the hard fullness that she entrapped. "You're so big," she breathed.

"And you're perfect for me. Tight and creamy." He groaned and lowered his face into the fragrant warmth of her neck. "Allison, I could come right now, but . . . but I'd like to . . . to love you first."

Her hands splayed wide over the rippling muscles of his back. "I want to experience it all, Spencer. Don't hold anything back."

Lifting his head, he sought her mouth with his as he began to move. At first his probings were tentative, but they soon became long, slow strokes that took him to the very gate of her womb.

In the depth of her femininity the spring that had so recently been released began to wind tight again. Incredulously, she blinked up at him as he braced himself over her with one arm. He smiled down on her and fondled her breast with his free hand. With each smooth thrust of his body, his fingertips brushed her nipple. Soon her head was tossing back and forth on the pillow and she was lifting herself to meet him.

"Spencer," she cried out when the waves of pleasure crashed over her again.

He reached as high as he could, clenching his teeth against the intensity of feeling that rushed into her body along with his fire.

Depleted, they lay entwined, her head lying in the crook of his elbow. From a distance of a few inches, their eyes locked.

"You're too far away," he complained.

"But if I lie any closer, I can't see you."

"It's a tough compromise," he conceded, his eyes wandering down her body. He chuckled softly.

"I'm that funny to look at?"

"No," he said, grasping her hand and bringing it to

his mouth for a kiss. "I just remembered a crude joke about how to tell a true redhead from a bottled one." Her complexion turned to a rosy hue all over and he laughed out loud. "I see you've heard it too."

"Yes, and it *is* crude."

A lazy finger trailed down her body and homed in on the vulnerable spot, where it languished. "But we know you're a true one, don't we?" He kissed her. As the kiss deepened, he molded his hand to her shape, cupping her mound tenderly. "It feels so good to be inside you."

"Where'd you come from anyway? All my life I've dreaded giving up my virginity because of the fear of pain. I didn't even feel it when you . . . uh . . ."

"You were busy," he said smugly.

She wanted to appear offended, but found herself laughing and cuddling closer to him. "I was, wasn't I?"

"Uh-huh. I think I know where the saying rocking the boat originated."

"Oh!" She sat up and swatted him on the thigh.

"Ouch!" He delighted in the bouncing of her breasts and the flare of temper in her flashing eyes. "I've already got several battle wounds."

"What? Where?"

"Ten crescent moon–shaped gouges on my buns. You really should trim your fingernails."

"What an indelicate, ungentlemanly thing to say!" she admonished, pushing her fists into her hips.

He took one adoring look at her indignant posture, then hauled her down and pinned her beneath him. "Don't get too saucy," he warned before kissing her soundly. "Besides, I know it's all an act. You put up this prim and prissy front when all the time you're a redheaded wildcat in bed."

She submitted to another kiss before looking up at him demurely. "I am?"

"You am." He pulled the sheet over them and cosseted her against him. "I've been meaning to ask you about that."

"About what?" She had gained enough confidence to tweak at his chest hair.

"Since you and Ann are identical, and you seemed to believe I was attracted to her, why didn't you think I'd be attracted to you?"

"Did you know that Ann and I have different birthdays?"

"I assume that question has something to do with what we're talking about."

"It does. She was born one minute before midnight on a Wednesday and I was born thirty seconds after midnight on Thursday."

"That explains everything," he said dryly.

"It does in a way. You know that rhyme about Monday's child, et cetera?"

"Yes."

"Okay, Wednesday's child, Ann, is in the know. Thursday's child, me, has far to go."

He leaned his head back and looked down his nose at her. "I interpret that to mean that a Thursday's child is bound for success. Not that I believe in that foolishness, you understand. I'm only carrying on this conversation to humor you and to pass the time while I'm regaining my strength."

She felt herself blushing and decided that it was a

curse that would follow her to the grave. Who would have thought she could still blush?

"I interpret it a different way," she said, drawing them back to the subject. "I think it means that Thursday's child has a long way to go to catch up with everyone else. At least that's proved to be the interpretation in my own life."

"Elaborate, please."

"Ann and I were identical, true, but things came easy for her. She could dance; I couldn't. She learned to play the piano like a virtuoso; I can barely read music. She got along with people. I didn't care for anyone's company as much as my own. Our mother wanted us to be perfect Southern ladies. Ann could pour tea for a party of twenty and not spill a drop. I was a calamity waiting to happen. Ann could lie and get away with murder. I've never been able to fib and got six spankings to her one. Do you see what I'm saying?"

"But you're twice as bright as Ann," he protested.

"People don't care how smart a woman is as long as she's charming and gay and pretty. Besides, we have the same I.Q. If Ann had applied herself to do the work I do, she probably would have won a Nobel prize by now."

He laughed, but hugged her tighter. "I hardly think that."

For several moments they were silent and reflective, then he said, "I suppose you transferred all these failures to your love life as well."

She propped herself up to lean over him and met his eyes levelly. "Exactly, Spencer. I knew Ann would most assuredly have a perfectly wonderful marriage and model children. I'd likely get left standing at the altar or something equally humiliating. Rather than venture into something that was doomed to failure, I didn't even try. I separated myself from men entirely, until—"

She stopped and her eyes flickered away. "Until me," he finished quietly.

"Yes."

"And I wouldn't let you retreat into that shell and hide behind those godawful clothes."

Her chin came up defiantly. "No, you wouldn't! You kept coming on and coming on. And now look at the mess you've gotten yourself into."

Rolling them over until he was on top again, he smiled down at her. "Yeah, just look. Boy, I'm in such a mess I can hardly stand it. See how much I'm suffering?" He positioned his body over hers so she would know his meaning. As her eyes went wide and foggy with renewed desire, he bent his head to kiss her neck. "Do you think I would have made a pest of myself, been so damned determined to have you, if I didn't see you as the most beautiful, desirable woman I'd ever met?"

Without preliminary—indeed, none was necessary—he entered her again. "Maybe you'd better . . . ah, Spencer, right there . . . keep repeating that so I'll . . . oh, God . . . remember it."

"I'll tell you so often you'll get sick of hearing it."

She folded her limbs around him and drew him deeper inside. "I doubt that, Spencer Raft. I doubt that very much."

The next five days aboard the *Double Dealer* were sun-washed and moon-kissed and love-steeped. Each morning

Spencer steered the yacht out into the ocean. "So we can cavort nekkid," he said with a leer, grabbing at her fanny with playful lechery.

When had nakedness become such a wonderful state? Allison wondered. She became quite at home with the condition. All her senses were awakened. She loved the feel of salt air blowing through her hair, or cooling their sweat-sheened bodies after a bout of feverish lovemaking. Food tasted delicious. She loved the sparkling tingle of wine on her tongue and the mingled fragrances of the sea and Spencer's after-shave.

Sometimes they went into Harbor Town for dinner, sometimes they picnicked on the deck, sometimes they shared a leisurely candlelit meal in the tiny galley.

One night they toured the island by car just for a change of scenery. Spencer believed in enjoying the scenery to the fullest, utilizing it. He found a private estate with a sprawling lawn that sloped down to the beach. By all appearances the family who occupied the house was away and had been for some time.

They got out of the car and strolled the beach hand in hand, watching the moon come up. The giant trees sheltered the lawn of the estate like a giant umbrella. As they were making their way back to the car, Spencer drew her into the purple shadow of a live oak that was laden with clumps of moss.

He leaned her against one low branch and kissed her with the passion she had come to know, the passion that never seemed to abate. His hand slipped under her skirt and toyed with the lace leg of her panties. When he began to pull them down, Allison freed her mouth and demanded, "What are you doing?"

"I think that's obvious." He bent his knees and took one of her breasts into his mouth, loving the nipple with his tongue through her sheer blouse. "Hmmm, Spencer, stop. Please, darling. We can't. Not here."

But she stepped free of the panties when he peeled them down her legs. And when he bent her back over the low limb, it received her as comfortably as an embracing arm. Then he was there, smooth and warm and hard . . . filling . . . pumping . . . loving . . .

So languid was she afterward that he swept her into his arms and carried her to the car.

"You have such influence over me," she mumbled against his throat.

"Good or bad?" he asked, chuckling.

Sighing, she replied, "I haven't decided. But whichever, I love it."

CHAPTER TEN

Before they left Hilton Head, Spencer stopped at the post office. Waiting for him in the general delivery box was a bundle of mail. As they took the highway back to Atlanta, Allison's curiosity got the best of her and she began reading the postmarks on the various envelopes. Denmark. Great Britain. Italy. Peru. The correspondence had come from all over the world.

She caught him watching her out of the corner of his eye. "Curiosity killed the cat, you know."

"I didn't ask." She tossed the mail over her shoulder onto the backseat of the car.

"No, but you wanted to." He laughed, laying a proprietary hand on her thigh and patting it.

They telephoned Ann the moment they arrived at Allison's apartment. Excitedly she related the news of their return to Davis and he suggested they all meet for dinner.

Allison and Spencer were already at the designated Italian restaurant when Ann and Davis arrived. Ann's eyes busily darted over her sister, taking in everything, especially the glowing complacency in her eyes. She wrapped Allison in a bear hug and whispered in her ear, "It was wonderful, wasn't it?"

Allison whispered back, "Yes, it was wonderful."

Davis's greeting was less effusive. He shook Spencer's hand enthusiastically enough, but the hug he gave Allison was restrained and stiff. It was the first time they'd seen each other since he'd found out about the sisters' switch.

"Uh, Allison, about, uh, about the way I, uh, you know—"

Ann jerked on his coattail and he dropped into the chair beside her. "For heaven's sake, Davis. It was only a few kisses and gropes."

He gulped, his face turning beet red. They all laughed, but Spencer draped a possessive arm around Allison's shoulder. "He'd just better not try it again."

Once Davis got over his embarrassment, they spent a gay evening together, eating pasta and veal and drinking wine. They were amazed at Allison's newfound tolerance of it.

"Spencer tutored me on how to make two glasses last all evening."

"I'll bet that's not all he tutored you on," Ann said suggestively.

Allison's cheeks warmed. Spencer raised her hand and kissed the backs of her fingers. "She taught me quite a bit too."

Ann and Davis had signed a contract on the house. Allison's intuition had been right. Ann had loved it.

They laughed over the realtor who had been confused when Ann dashed through the house animatedly remarking on each feature as though she'd never seen it before.

"I want to do that master bathroom in peach and mint. What do you think, Allison?"

"I think it'll be lovely." Beneath the table, Spencer was squeezing her knee.

"Just think, darling," Ann said, laying her head on Davis's shoulder, "it won't be long before we'll live there."

Allison joined the clandestine loveplay going on beneath the red-and-white-checked tablecloth. She adjusted Spencer's napkin on his lap, smoothed out imaginary wrinkles, adjusted it again, patted it into place.

"Can you believe the wedding's only four weeks—"

Suddenly Spencer jumped up, bumping against the table in his haste. "I can't believe it's after midnight and I haven't tucked Allison into bed yet. Good night, you two."

They rushed out, leaving Ann and Davis mystified.

They spent two nights in Allison's apartment. She never actually invited him to stay with her. It seemed to have been preordained.

On Sunday, the twins, with Davis and Spencer, attended church with the Leamons. Afterward Mr. Leamon invited them all out for brunch. Her parents' gushing hospitality toward Spencer embarrassed Allison.

"You'd think I was a forty-year-old spinster they had tried to marry off for years," she complained when they returned to his car. "I think if you'd made a move like you were going to run, Daddy would have tackled you."

"The only move I want to make is this one." He drew

her tight against him and delivered a kiss that enflamed her body and sent her spirit soaring. For the rest of the afternoon they made leisurely love, dozed, made love again.

It wasn't until much later, after the sun had set, that the bubble burst. She was returning to the bedroom after having gone into the kitchen to get them something to drink. At first she wondered what his suitcase was doing on the bed. Then the reason blared through her head like the blast of a trumpet. The tray in her hands began to shake and she set it on the bedside table.

Spencer was folding his clothes and packing them neatly. "Where are you going?" she asked inanely. What did his destination matter? He was leaving. She had thought that she would welcome the moment he left so she wouldn't have to dread it anymore. But now that it was here, she couldn't conceive of ever having wished for it. She thought she might die of the pain.

"I have to go back to Hilton Head tonight."

"I see."

He dropped a shirt into the suitcase and straightened to look at her. "No, you don't." His voice was as gentle as the hands that pressed the top of her shoulders until she was sitting on the side of the bed. He knelt in front of her. Taking both her hands in his, he studied them, rubbing her knuckles, charting the veins with his fingertip.

She wanted to tear her hands out of his grasp and away from this tenderness. Why was he letting her down gently? Did he think it would hurt any less if he was kind rather than cruel?

"Allison, I have important business that needs tending

to. You saw that stack of mail. I have to go back and secure the *Double Dealer,* then fly to New York tomorrow."

Well, she wasn't going to collapse into tears. If that's
what he expected, he was in for a disappointment. If she
had learned anything from him, it was that she was a
woman worthy of a man's loving attention. She'd be
damned before she'd grovel or beg. He had helped her
throw off that shell of self-consciousness she'd hidden
behind for years. She didn't want it back. Life without it
had been too good.

"You don't owe me any explanations, Spencer."

He heard the tartness in her voice and his lips thinned
in irritation. "Yes, I do. Did you think I was just going to
walk out without a word?"

She raised rebellious eyes to his. "I don't know. Were
you?"

"Damn!" he said, coming to his feet. He paced the
length of the bed, combing through his hair with frustrated fingers. Men really hated scenes like this. They
wanted clean breaks, no looking back, no tears or re-
criminations. "Why are you making this so difficult?"

"I'm not," she said, springing off the bed. "You have
to go, so go."

"I have to go, yes. But I don't want to. Not like this.
Not with things unsettled between us."

"As far as I'm concerned, they are settled. You fulfilled your end of the bargain."

"What's that supposed to mean?"

"You did your part of the fertilization process. Thank
you for being so conscientious and thorough."

He muttered words she had only seen scrawled on

public rest-room walls, never spoken aloud. "Is that all this last week meant to you?"

No, no, her heart screamed. Couldn't he see that she was disintegrating on the inside? Didn't he know that she'd given little thought to becoming pregnant and that every act of love had been just that, love? Had he been with so many women, spent so many idyllic weeks like the one just past, that he didn't recognize the real thing?

"You know why I went to Hilton Head with you." She spoke the untruthful words softly because she could barely get them past the lump in her throat.

He muttered another series of scathing oaths, then swung back to the suitcase. He closed it with a resounding snap. The finality of that sound went through her like a bullet.

"I won't be able to contact you for a while. I'll be in New York, then possibly Turkey."

Turkey? My God. So far away. Another world. They truly did move in separate realms, didn't they? Whatever had made her think he would be content with her?

He stalked to the front door, paused, and looked back at her. He seemed to want to say so much. All he said was, "Good-bye, Allison."

"Good-bye." *My love,* she added under her breath as the screen door slammed shut behind him.

Dr. Hyden's eyes expressed his surprise and delight in the changes in her. The moment she came through the lab door he said, "Well, well, look at you! Is that a new dress?"

"Yes," she said tersely, going to the portable closet to

store her handbag. She might just as well get used to this. Everyone would be curious to know what had happened to her budding love affair.

"And how is our Mr. Raft after a week's vacation?" Dr. Hyden asked, rocking back on his heels and winking at her.

"He was fine the last time I saw him," she said with studied indifference. Dr. Hyden's ebullience collapsed so suddenly that had the circumstances not been so grim, Allison would have laughed. "He's off to parts unknown. I'll probably never see him again."

"But I thought——"

"What? That we were *involved?* Heavens, no," she said breezily. "It was just a lark. How is Rasputin? Did he miss me?" She effectively dismissed the subject of Spencer Raft for the time being and Dr. Hyden left her, shaking his head in dismay.

Ann's dismay was even harder to cope with. She telephoned as soon as Allison got home from work.

"Davis said Spencer called him last night on his way out of town."

"Did he?" Allison asked coolly.

"For heaven's sake, Allison, what's going on?"

"Nothing. He had to leave. You know he's a world traveler. Surely you didn't expect him to hang around for long?"

"But . . . he . . . you . . . I thought, Davis and I both thought, that the two of you——"

"No, of course not. It was nothing permanent. Just one of those fleeting things. Ann, I've got to run. My kettle is boiling over."

For weeks she adroitly avoided conversations about

Spencer, ignored speculative glances and dodged probing questions. But that didn't stop her from thinking about him. He stalked her during the day and haunted her at night. She ached for his caresses, but more than that, she wanted to be again the woman she was with him, gay, witty, eloquent, beautiful. Tennyson had been wrong. It wasn't better to have loved and lost. Now she knew what she was missing, and the misery of doing without him was almost too much to bear.

She was angry with him for leaving, and angry with herself for worrying about him. Where was he? Was he safe? Was he in danger? What possible business could he have in Turkey? *Turkey,* for godsakes!

The week she was to have her menstrual period came and went and nothing happened. She dared not hope. There were a multitude of reasons why she might be late, foremost, her emotional instability. But another week went by, then another.

The Friday before Ann's wedding, after everyone had left the lab, she ran a pregnancy test on herself. The results were conclusively positive.

Only then did she cry. She had not wept one tear for Spencer, not a single tear for her broken heart, her lost love, her empty life. But now she buried her head in her arms and wept for over an hour.

The tears cleansed her mind and her system. When at last she raised her head and dried her eyes, she knew a peace that she'd never known before.

She had done something right! She was going to have a baby, a wonderful, intelligent, beautiful baby. It was hers. And she would pour into it all the love Spencer had given her, enough to last a lifetime in the space of a week.

•   •   •

She tripped on the plastic bag her bridesmaid's dress was wrapped in as she raced up the steps of the church. She was late and Ann would kill her. Thank God none of the guests were arriving yet. She had slept right through her alarm and had had to rush through her bath and shampoo and manicure. Her right thumbnail was smeared, but hopefully no one would notice.

The inside foyer was dim and it took her eyes a moment to adjust. Then, getting her bearings, she started down the deserted corridor looking for the bride's changing room.

A side exit swung open and a man's silhouette filled the doorway before the door closed behind him. "Excuse me, miss, I'm looking for—"

They both came to an abrupt halt as they stood facing each other. She hadn't known whether to expect him to be here or not. He hadn't been at the rehearsal last night, and, as though he had recently died, no one had mentioned his name to her.

He had his suitcase under one arm and was carrying a tuxedo over his shoulder by a crooked finger. He was disheveled and appeared to have been rushed. His jeans and running shoes looked out of place in the staid church hallway. His hair was windblown and the sunglasses he usually wore had been shoved to the top of his head. He looked tired and haggard. The lines in his face were more pronounced.

But to the woman gazing up at him, he was the most beautiful sight in the world.

And she became mortifyingly aware that she looked

like hell. She had rolled her hair on electric curlers before leaving home. The pins were sticking out around her head like antennas. Because she still hadn't applied her eye makeup, she was wearing her glasses. She had on a pair of jeans that had belonged to her since high school and a misshapen T-shirt she'd stolen from the box of clothing her mother had designated for Goodwill.

"Hello, Allison."

"Hello," she said in a voice she wished had sounded ten times more confident.

"I'm late."

"So am I."

"I just flew in from New York."

"Oh. How was your trip?"

"Long and tiring."

His eyes remained steadily on her, piercing and incisive. "Uh, well, I have to get dressed. I'm sure Ann is—"

"Wait a minute." He managed to wedge her between himself and the wall. "I want to know."

She licked her lips. "Want to know what?"

"Are you carrying my baby?"

What had she expected? Tact? Subtlety? From this man? No way. She cast a furtive glance up and down the hall, hoping that no one was eavesdropping. When she ran out of things to look at, she had no choice but to lift her eyes back to his.

He was so . . . so *everything* any woman could want. She felt just the way she had the first time she looked at him with clear vision—weightless, lost, powerless, incomplete. Only now added to those sensations was an infinite sadness, because she knew firsthand that every emotion he inspired, he also fulfilled.

Perhaps he did care about the child. Perhaps he did hold some affection for her. But he was what he was, and she was what she was, and any lasting relationship had been hopeless from the beginning. She had always known that. That she carried his life within her didn't alter the facts of their lives. Even if he stayed with her out of a sense of obligation, would that be fair to either of them? He would come to resent her for tying him down and she would come to resent his restlessness.

He would have to know the truth in due time, but she would never use the child as a means to hold him.

I love you, Spencer. For that reason, good-bye, my love.

"No," she said. "There's no child."

A door down the hall was thrown open. It banged against the wall and they both jumped. Davis came striding out, looking like the stereotypically frantic bridegroom a few minutes before the wedding.

"Spencer, thank God you're here. I was about to send a police escort to the airport for you. Good heavens, Allison, aren't you dressed yet?"

"No," she said, edging past Spencer. "And I'd better hurry or Ann will never speak to me again." She scurried down the hall, but her rapid footsteps belied her spirit, which seemed shackled to her like a ball and chain.

"Do you, Davis Harrington Lundstrum, take this woman to be your lawfully wedded wife . . ."

The minister intoned the vows and Davis and Ann responded in hushed tones in keeping with the sanctity of the occasion. The candles flickered only slightly. The scent of summer flowers permeated the chapel. The afternoon sun shone through the stained-glass windows like a divine blessing.

Allison was aware only of the blue eyes that stared at her, burning hotter and steadier than any of the candles. She knew the peach-colored silk dress was flattering to her complexion. She knew that the style, with its scooped neckline and narrow waist, did her figure no harm. She knew that beneath the matching straw hat her hair gleamed.

But was that any reason for the best man to stare fixedly at her, to look like he was about to explode from some internal combustion, to look like at any moment he would shove minister, bride, and groom aside and reach for her?

Even during the singing of "The Lord's Prayer," which must be the longest song ever composed, his intense stare didn't waver. The bride and groom kept their heads reverently bowed. But each time Allison peeped at the best man through her lashes, she met the compelling heat of those blue eyes that seemed to glow brighter with each passing minute.

If he had wanted to ruin Ann's wedding for her, he succeeded. She would never remember a moment of it. When the minister said, "You may now kiss your bride," she jumped as if a hypnotist had just snapped her out of a trance.

She returned Ann's bouquet and, as rehearsed, bride and groom linked arms and went down the aisle together, beaming their happiness on each other and their guests. Someone must have cued Spencer on his part, for he crooked his right arm and Allison had no choice but to link her left one through it and let him escort her down the aisle.

When they reached the vestibule, he spun her around to face him, backed her into the wall, and said, "I have two questions."

The photographer was urging the wedding party toward the limousines parked outside waiting to drive them to the country club for the reception.

"Be right with you," Spencer told him over his shoulder, but neither his hands nor his eyes released Allison. "Two questions."

"Everyone's coming out of the chapel, Spencer."

"Two questions," he barked.

"All right, but whisper, please."

He decreased his volume, but not his determination. "One. Are you pregnant with my child?"

"I told you no."

"You're no damn good at lying, Allison."

She glanced over the bulwark of his shoulder to see her parents, Davis's, and other wedding guests glancing at them curiously. "You shouldn't cuss in church."

He shook her slightly. "Answer me and remember I'll know if you're lying."

Her eyes traveled over the front of his tux, then up to his face, finally lighting guiltily on his eyes. "Yes." She saw an emotion streak through his eyes. Unsure of what it was, she rushed on. "I meant to tell you, only not—"

"Two. Do you love me?"

Her mouth was already open, ready to explain why she had lied to him before, but anything she might have said stalled in her throat. "What did you say?"

He took a step closer. The emphatic tone in his voice tempered and became one of uncertainty. "Do you love me, Allison?"

It was the humility behind the question that undid her, that endearing, heart-wrenching, helpless quality in his voice that was so totally unlike him. All the strength and resolve deserted her and she wilted toward him. "You'll know if I lie?"

"You're a terrible liar."

"I love you, Spencer."

They fell into each other's arms, hugging each other tight, swaying slightly. "That's what I had to know. What I wanted to hear." Finally he set her away from him and grabbed her hand. "Come on."

He dragged her out the door, her flustered parents in their wake. The bride and groom were standing beside the limousine, watching their attendants as they ran pell-mell down the church steps.

"Hey, where are you going?" Davis called. Spencer had ignored the limousines and was making his way toward a car parked across the street.

Impatiently he retraced their steps and shook Davis's hand heartily. "Great wedding, friend. Ann"—he kissed her soundly on surprised lips—"best wishes."

"B—but where are you going?" Davis asked when Spencer once again headed for the other car.

"Wait here," he instructed Allison, who mindlessly obeyed him even though he'd left her standing in the middle of the street. He virtually hurdled the hood of the limousine to get back to Davis. He whispered something in Davis's ear, then ran back to Allison, recaptured her hand, and hustled her into the car.

After they had sped away, Ann turned to Davis and asked the question paramount in everyone's mind. "What did he tell you? Where are they going?"

Davis tugged at his bowtie and cast an apologetic smile at the Leamons. "He said, we'd had the wedding, but they were taking the honeymoon."

When they stepped aboard the *Double Dealer,* she was still in her bridesmaid's dress, he in his tux, though he'd taken off the bow tie and his shirt was unbuttoned. Allison had entertained herself on the trip by pulling out the studs one by one and running her hand over his bare chest as he drove.

"You're gonna get us both killed."

"Okay, I'll stop," she had said.

"Don't you dare." He had taken her hand and pressed it over his heart.

Now, he led her down the steps into the cabin below the deck. They left the lights off as they turned to each other and came together in an eager embrace.

His arms went around her tightly. She plunged her hands beneath the tuxedo jacket and spread them wide over his back. Their mouths kissed ravenously, without technique or patience. They were greedy for the taste of the other and appeasing that craving was uppermost.

When they fell apart to breathe, he settled his mouth over her ear. "Will you marry me?"

"After you abducted me from church in front of all those people? I'll have to or be branded a scarlet woman."

His tongue bathed her earlobe. "Would you anyway?"

"Yes," she admitted on a shuddering sigh as his hand moved up from her waist to fondle her breast. While she still retained a modicum of sanity, she pushed him away. "On one condition."

"What's that?" he said, shrugging off his jacket.

"You tell me what you do for a living."

With a heavy sigh, he tossed the jacket onto a chair. For a long moment he hung his head, his hair falling over his brow. When he raised his head, his eyes were bleak. "You're not going to like it, Allison." He shook his head in resignation. "But I guess I'll have to show you my cache."

Her hands found each other at her waist and gripped hard. "Cache?"

"Yeah. Where I keep the goods."

First switching on a lamp, he went to a wall of cabinets and squatted in front of one. When he swung open the door, Allison saw a stainless-steel safe built into the wall.

Her heart began to pound as he worked the combination. He cranked the handle down and pulled the safe open. She was prepared to see anything, cylinders of uranium, spacecraft blueprints, packets of cocaine. She held her breath as he pulled out one of several long, flat black boxes that could have been jewelry boxes. Stolen jewelry?

He extended it toward her. "This is what I trade in."

Her hands shaking, she opened the spring catch. Several seconds ticked by while she stared down at the contents.

"Stamps?" Lifting her disbelieving eyes to his, she repeated on a high squeak, "Stamps?"

"Not just stamps," he said huffily. "I'll have you know those are—"

"*Stamps!*" she shouted incredulously.

He pulled himself up to his full height. "I'm a philatelist. A stamp collector."

Still holding the box in which rested four stamps, she collapsed on the bed in vast relief. She began to laugh. "What's the big secret? Why do you hide what you do?"

"Because I'd get the same reaction from everyone as I've gotten from you. You have to admit, it's not a very macho occupation."

"Davis thinks that you're . . . well, you know what he thinks."

"So do most of my friends. Why disillusion them? If they want to think I traffic in something shady and live just beyond the pale, what harm is there?"

"I can't believe it."

"Disappointed?"

"Of course not. It's just . . ." She gazed around the interior of the yacht, where no expense had been spared. "Is there a living to be made from it?"

He grinned and lowered his voice. "I'm not an aesthete. I'm not motivated by a grand passion to possess rare stamps, as most collectors are."

"Then why do it?"

"Money," he said, his eyes twinkling. "I make it my business to find out when a collector is ready to sell. I buy the stamp, keep it a few years, let it appreciate, then turn around and sell it to a collector who has dedicated his life to possessing it and is willing to pay an astronomical price. Of course, some of the profit has to go into buying others. This isn't my entire inventory. The really valuable ones are in a vault in New York. Those you're holding are only worth several hundred thousand dollars."

Her mouth fell open as she stared down at the box again. "Several hundred thousand . . . for four stamps?"

"Will you stop saying *stamps* in that tone of voice? You don't lick these and stick them on a postcard, you know. They're considered works of art."

"I'm not denigrating them. I'm just—" She suddenly lunged off the bed. "I'm furious with you for letting me think you were involved in something dreadful."

He took the box from her and relocked the safe. "Calm down, Red. Are you gonna marry me or not?"

Grabbing handfuls of his hair, she gave his head a stern shake. "I guess I will. You still look like a ruthless pirate or mercenary."

"Thanks, I think. But the only thing I'm ruthless about is loving you."

"Will you always be going off to places like Turkey and leaving me alone for months at a time?"

"I've been making some plans. Much to the delight of my clients, who have had to chase me all over the globe for years, I'll open a permanent office. It may just as well be in Atlanta, since your work is there and it's near our families. You'll have to meet my parents soon, by the way. They'll like you."

"Get back to the plans."

"Oh yes, the plans. I'll hire a courier to make deliveries. But you and baby can go with me if a trade takes me to an interesting place."

"That's wonderful."

He had plucked her clothes from her as easily as playing "She loves me, she loves me not" with the petals of a daisy. His hands were appreciating her nakedness, roaming everywhere, touching, caressing, telling her how much he had missed the feel of her skin.

"What's wonderful?" he murmured against her neck.

"My plans or this?" Cupping her breasts, he dipped his head and sponged the tips with his nimble tongue.

"Both."

He kissed her breasts as though rediscovering their taste, then kissed his way down until he was kneeling in front of her. He opened his hands over the lower part of her body. "I can't wait to see you swollen with my baby." His mouth paid sweet tribute to her femininity.

"I can't wait to be either." Her head stretched backward from an arched throat as his adoration increased in fervor. "I'll give you a perfectly wonderful child, Spencer."

"I know you will. And I'll love him almost as much as I love his mother." Rising, he lifted her onto the bed and covered her with his body. "You didn't undress," she panted between kisses.

"I don't think I can wait."

"I don't think I can either." She sighed her pleasure as he stroked the moist warmth between her thighs. He parted and explored and loved her with his fingers.

She spread his shirt aside and raised her head to kiss his chest, flicking her tongue over his hardening nipples.

"Damn," he said between his teeth as her hands caressed down his stomach. "Are you the virgin I brought here just a few weeks ago?"

"The very same." She unbuckled his belt and unfastened his trousers. The hiss of the zipper was no less raspy than his breath when her fingers furrowed the dense hair that housed his sex.

"You wouldn't even touch me then."

"I was shy of you."

"Are you still shy of me, Allison?"

"No, never again. I love you."

"Do you?" He groaned when she took him fully.

"Yes."

"Show me."

And she did.

ABOUT THE AUTHOR

SANDRA BROWN began her writing career in 1980. After selling her first book, she wrote a succession of romance novels under several pseudonyms, most of which remain in print. She has become one of the country's most popular novelists, earning the notice of Hollywood and of critics. More than forty of her books have appeared on the *New York Times* best-seller list. There are fifty million copies of her books in print, and her work has been translated into twenty-nine languages. Prior to writing, she worked in commercial television as an on-air personality for *PM Magazine* and local news in Dallas. The parents of two, she and her husband now divide their time between homes in Texas and South Carolina.

Coming soon . . .

THE RANA LOOK

A passionate romance from
#1 *New York Times* bestselling
author Sandra Brown,
available for the first time
in hardcover in December 2002.

She was a model looking to restart her life . . .
he was a pro football star looking to restart
his career. But when reluctantly thrown together
as neighbors in a small Texas boardinghouse,
it is their romance that gets a jump-start. . . .

Read on for a preview. . . .

She met him in the hallway on her way down to dinner.

He was the last kind of surprise she expected. His impact on her was startling. Several things happened at once. She drew in a quick, sudden breath. Her heart slammed into her ribs. She flattened herself against the wall.

"Hi. Did I scare you?" he asked with a smile.

His teeth were white and straight. His easy grin lit up a darkly tanned, weathered face. When his lips tilted up at the corners, one dark brow tipped down, while the other arched high, as though reaching for the wavy lock of sable brown hair that had fallen across his forehead.

It was an intriguing smile. Arresting. Sexy. Her heart was pounding abnormally.

"N-no," she stammered.

"Didn't Aunt Ruby tell you she was getting a new boarder?"

"Yes, but I . . ."

She didn't finish. She couldn't very well say, "Yes, but I pictured a doddering elderly man with a pipe and cardigan, not one whose shoulders practically span the hallway." She had expected the new boarder to have a benevolent face with a pleasant smile. Not one that made her think of daredevils and ne'er-do-wells.

Still smiling, he set down the box of records and tapes he had been holding under his right arm and extended his hand to her. "Trent Gamblin."

Rana stared at his hand for an embarrassing length of time before laying hers against it, not quite clasping it, and muttering, "I'm Miss Ramsey."

When she dared to raise her eyes to his, his smile had deepened. She suspected that he was smiling with derision at her primness.

"Do you need any assistance, Mr. Gamblin?" she asked starchily as she drew her hand back.

"I think I can handle it, Miss Ramsey." His face was solemn now, but the mirth was still twinkling in his eyes. They were the color of coffee liqueur, dark and rich and fluid.

Slightly irked that he apparently found her so amusing, she pried herself away from the wall and stood up straight. "Then if you'll excuse me, I'll go on down for dinner. Ruby gets cross if I'm late for meals."

"Guess I'd better hurry down too. Left or right?"

"Pardon?"

"Which apartment is mine? The one on the left or the one on the right?"

"The left."

"The right one is yours?"

"Yes."

"I sure hope I can keep that straight, Miss Ramsey. I'd hate to come stumbling into your room some night by mistake." His mischievous eyes traveled over her. "No telling what might happen."

He was laughing at her! "I'll see you downstairs," she said coolly. She marched past him, forcing him to press himself up against the wall to let her pass. But he didn't press quite far enough. As she went past him, her clothes dragged against the front of his. He did it on purpose, of course. She could feel his arrogant smile at her back.

If only he knew, she fumed silently as she took the stairs. Miss Ramsey could dazzle him, freeze him in his tracks, wipe that tomcat grin right off his smug face—

Rana paused on the third step from the bottom. Why was she even entertaining such thoughts? She hadn't cared about her appearance for months. All that was behind her. Why now, after meeting the new boarder in Mrs. Ruby Bailey's house, was she even thinking of the Rana she had been six months before?

She disliked herself for it. She had cut herself off completely from her former life. She wasn't ready to resume it, not even temporarily, in order to put the conceited Trent Gamblin in his place.

Becoming the internationally known Rana again would bring back all the self-doubt and pain that went with the single name. She had given up her celebrity status. For the time being she didn't want it back. She was enjoying the anonymity of her current life too much. She liked being simply Miss Ramsey, an undistinguished resident of a typical Galveston boarding house.

Ruby Bailey, however, was about as atypical a landlady as one could imagine. When Rana entered the dining room, Ruby was lighting the candles she had placed in the center of the table. In honor of the new arrival, she had gone to special pains with the centerpiece this evening.

"Damn!" she exclaimed, fanning out the match. "I

almost caught my nail polish on fire." She inspected the crimson enamel on her nails.

Her age had never been firmly established, but Rana had calculated that it must be beyond seventy, judging from the dated references Ruby occasionally let slip in her colorful dialogue. She was hardly what Rana had pictured when she had responded to the ad in the Houston newspaper advertising an apartment for lease in Galveston.

With the directions Ruby had given her during a brief telephone interview, Rana had located the house without difficulty. Her excitement could barely be contained when she pulled up to the address. The Victorian house, built in Galveston's heyday, had withstood hurricanes as well as the ravages of time. It was situated on a tree-shaded street among other recently restored homes. For Rana, who had lived for the past decade in Manhattan's high rises, it was like stepping into another century. She was delighted. She only hoped she and Ruby Bailey would hit it off.

The landlady's hair was white, but it hadn't been pulled into the classic grandmother's bun, as Rana had imagined. Ruby wore it short and curly, cut in a surprisingly fashionable style. She wasn't matronly-plump, either, another misconception on Rana's part, but whipcord-lean. Her attire, far from conservative, consisted of a pair of jeans and a sweater the color of the vibrant red geraniums that bloomed in the concrete urns on the front porch.

"You could do with a good meal or two." That blunt statement was the first thing Ruby had said to Rana upon giving her an inspection with busy, no-nonsense brown eyes that could have snapped a longshoreman to attention. "Come on in. We'll start with sugar cookies and herbal tea. Do you like herbal tea? I swear by it. It's good for everything from toothache to constipation. Of course, if you eat the balanced meals I plan on cooking for you, you won't ever be constipated."

And that, it seemed, was that. Ruby considered the apartment on her second floor leased.

Rana would come to learn that Ruby's cup of herbal tea was sometimes liberally laced with Jack Daniel's, especially in the evening after dinner. Rana forgave her friend that particular idiosyncrasy, the same way she forgave Ruby the frown she made no effort to disguise as she looked up now and spotted Rana.

"I was hoping you'd gussy up a bit tonight. Your hair's such a pretty auburn color. Did you ever think of pulling it back away from your face a tad?"

Rana, darling your cheekbones are to die for! Show them off, love. I see all this glorious hair, sweeping back, big, big volumes of it, like a mane surrounding your face and cascading down your back. Shake your head, darling. See! Oh God, positively to die for! Every tacky little beauty shop in the country will soon be advertising the Rana Look.

Rana smiled at the memory of the famous hairdresser's words the first time Morey sent her to him. "No, Ruby, I like it like this." Ruby had insisted on being addressed by her first name, because she said being referred to as Mrs. Bailey made her feel old. "The table looks lovely tonight."

"Thank you," Ruby said impatiently as she spied a smear of paint on Rana's sleeve. "You have time to change, dear," she ventured tactfully.

"Does it matter what I'm wearing?"

Ruby sighed with resignation. "I suppose it doesn't. You'd only put on another of your horrid baggy combinations, none of which I'd be caught dead in, and I have about three decades on you. I'm sure, Miss Ramsey, that you could make yourself more attractive if only you'd try." First names didn't apply to her guests.

"I'm not interested in my appearance."

Ruby assessed Rana's flat, functional shoes, her shapeless dress, and the heavy hair hanging on either side of her thin face, a face made to appear even more gaunt by oversized round eyeglasses. Ruby's disapproving expression clearly said, "That's readily apparent." Her actual words were, "Trent's just arrived."

"Yes, I met him upstairs."

Ruby's brown eyes sparkled. "Isn't he the most adorable boy you've ever seen?"

"I didn't expect him to be so . . . young." So young, so good-looking, so virile, and so dangerous to have around, Rana added to herself. What if he recognized her? "I thought you said the new boarder was your cousin."

"Nephew, dear, nephew. He's always been a favorite of mind. My sister spoiled him abominably. Of course I constantly chastised her for it. But she couldn't help herself. Who could? He could twist any woman around his little finger. When he called and said he needed a place to stay for the next few weeks, I pretended to be aggravated, but actually I was delighted. He'll be such fun to have around."

"It's only for a few weeks?"

"Yes, and then he'll move back into his house in Houston."

Divorce, no doubt, Rana thought. This nephew of

Ruby's, this Trent, needed a place to stay while waiting for a nasty divorce to become final. Well, Aunt Ruby might think he was an "adorable boy," but Rana knew an arrogant, conceited, sexist chauvinist when she saw one. She had every intention of staying out of Mr. Adorable's way. It wouldn't be difficult. A man like Trent Gamblin would never look twice at a woman like "Miss Ramsey."

"Something smells wonderful."

Rana actually jumped at the sound of his cello-mellow voice as he came striding through the portiere that hung across the doorway. His sure footsteps thudded on the hardwood floor. Each strike of his boot heels made the floorboards groan and the china and glass bric-a-brac tinkle against each other.

Ruby was encircled from behind by a pair of brawny brown arms that Michelangelo would have loved to sculpt. Trent bent over her spare body and nuzzled her neck. "Whatcha got cookin', Auntie?"

"Let me go, you big gorilla." She wriggled out of his suffocating embrace, but her cheeks were flushed and her eyes were more animated than usual. "Sit down and behave. Did you wash your hands before coming downstairs?"

"Yes, ma'am," he said meekly, winking slyly at Rana at the same time.

"If you can mind your manners, I'll let you sit at the head of the table. Ask her nicely and Miss Ramsey might pour some sherry for you. Now, excuse me and I'll bring dinner out."

With her electric-blue skirt rustling, Ruby sashayed through the swinging door into the kitchen. When Trent turned around, he was still grinning in approval of his saucy elderly aunt. "She's something, isn't she?" he asked Rana.

"Yes, she is. I like her immensely."

"She's outlived three husbands and one daughter. But none of that got her down." He shook his head in perplexed admiration. "Where do you sit?"

Rana moved toward her accustomed place setting, but he rounded the table with the grace of a *danseur noble* and moved her chair away from the table for her.

Rana was tall. He was much taller. It was odd, and disconcertingly pleasant, to have a man tower over her. Even if she were wearing the highest high heels, Trent Gamblin would be taller than she.

When she was seated in the rosewood lyre-back chair, he took his place at the head of the table. "How long have you lived here?"

"Six months."

"Before that?"

"Back East," she answered obliquely.

He grinned broadly. "I didn't think that was a Texas accent."

She laughed softly. "Hardly." To keep from looking at him, she toyed with her spoon, tracing the elaborate silver pattern with the pad of her middle finger.

"Did you know the other boarder?"

"Guest."

"Huh?"

"Your aunt calls us guests. She says 'boarder' sounds too commercial."

"Ahh." He nodded. His throat was brown and strong. His shirt was opened at the collar, and Rana could see a healthy crop of curling dark hair in the V. Looking at it made her stomach feel weightless, so she averted her eyes. "I'll have to rely on you to acquaint me with the house rules. What time is curfew?"

He was teasing again, and, as before, it annoyed her. She had known plenty of men who played these kinds of flirting games, some of them with more talent than Trent Gamblin. They were games in which a woman was inevitably the prey and a man the hunter. Rana had always resented the masculine assumption that she was interested in such tiresome silliness. She did so now.

Besides, why was this man playing the game with the homely Miss Ramsey?

Then the answer came to her. Except for his aunt, Rana was the only woman around. If there was one aspect of Mr. Gamblin's personality that was readily apparent, it was that he was a born womanizer. Habits were hard to break.

"The former occupant of your apartment was a widow about Ruby's age," Rana explained briskly. "When her health declined, she went to live in Austin, nearer her family."

She took a dainty sip from her water glass, a gesture that she hoped would suspend conversation until their hostess brought in dinner. The dining room seemed awfully close and stuffy this evening. She ruled out the possibility that Trent Gamblin's presence had anything to do with it. Perhaps Ruby needed to adjust the thermostat on the air-conditioner.

Disobeying his aunt's instructions to mind his manners, Trent propped his elbow on the table and rested his chin in his hand while he unabashedly studied Miss Ramsey.

Interesting. She couldn't be very old. Either side of thirty by a year or two. She mystified him. Why would a seemingly healthy, intelligent young woman ensconce herself permanently in Aunt Ruby's boarding house, quaint and charming though it was? What would motivate a woman to isolate herself deliberately?

Family tragedy, perhaps? A love affair gone awry? Had she been jilted at the altar or something equally shattering?

Miss Ramsey made him think of nothing so much as a spinster schoolmarm of a hundred years ago. Thin face, lank hair—although the candlelight made it shine a color like nothing he'd ever seen before—that awful gray dress that kept her figure a total secret even from his discerning eyes. She wore no makeup, but her complexion was clear. Unlike that of most redheads, her skin had an olive tint. Actually, though, her hair was too dark just to be called "red." That deep mahogany luster went far beyond merely red.

Her hands, which kept fidgeting with her silverware, were amazingly small and long-fingered, but looked rough. Her nails had been cut bluntly at the ends of her fingers. She was wearing no polish on them. Nor was she wearing perfume. His nose could detect and name at least fifty different fragrances. Miss Ramsey wasn't wearing one of them. What he hated most were her round eyeglasses. Their blue-tinted lenses hid her eyes completely.

His steady, bold stare was making her nervous. He could tell by the way she kept shifting in her chair. In a mischievous way, he was glad his attention was unsettling her. The poor thing probably needed a thrill or two to enliven her dull, drab existence. If he could oblige, why not? He had nothing better to do.

"Why are you living here, Miss Ramsey?"

"None of your business."

"Ouch! Are you always so prickly?"

"Only when someone is rude enough to stare and ask nosy questions."

"I'm the new kid on the block. You're supposed to be nice to me."

Aunt Ruby's bragging wasn't without some basis. He *was* adorable, particularly when he formed that boyish pout that somehow looked just right on his sensual lips.

"Would you like some sherry?" Rana lifted the lead-crystal decanter.

"Are you serious?" She set it back down. "Got a cold Coors?"

"I don't think Ruby stocks beer."

"I'll bet she's never out of whiskey, though."

Rana's cheeks went red. "I don't—"

"Come on, now, Miss Ramsey. You can tell me. I'm family." He leaned forward conspiratorially, moving his face to within scant inches of hers. "Does the old girl still swizzle her Jack Daniel's?"

Before Rana could form a response, Ruby appeared, pushing a tea cart loaded with silver platters through the kitchen door. "Here we are, dears. I'm sure you're starving, but the rolls needed a few more minutes in the oven."

Trent, still staring at Rana's shocked expression, chuckled softly.

"Trent, stop that irritating sniggering," Ruby scolded. "You always were the rudest child at the table and prone to laugh for no apparent reason. Sit up straight, please, and make yourself useful by carving this roast for me. Miss Ramsey likes hers medium-to-well done, and be generous with her portion despite her protests. I've managed to put some meat on her meager bones, but she still has a long way to go. Now, isn't this nice?" Ruby said enthusiastically as she took her seat. "This is going to be so cozy, the three of us sharing every meal."

Rana, who was trying to ignore Trent's calculating assessment of just how meager her bones were, was wondering if it would be too obvious if she asked to have her meals in her apartment from now on.

Trent had a hefty appetite. Ruby kept refilling his plate, until he held up his hands in surrender after eating two and a half portions of everything.

"Please, Aunt Ruby, no more. I'll go to fat."

"Nonsense. You're still a growing boy. I can't send you to summer camp weak and unfit."

Rana choked on a bite of parsleyed potatoes and took a quick drink of water. Her eyes brimmed with tears, but she was careful not to remove her glasses as she blotted them.

"Are you all right, dear?" Ruby asked with concern.

"Fine, fine," Rana choked out. When she was composed, she looked at Trent. "Aren't you a little old to be sent off to summer camp?"

Ruby and Trent both found that highly amusing, and they laughed heartily. "Football summer camp," Ruby explained. "Didn't I tell you that Trent is a professional football player?"

Rana, embarrassed, smoothed her napkin back in her lap. "I don't believe you did."

"He plays with the Houston Mustangs." Ruby beamed proudly, laying her hand on her nephew's muscled arm. "And he's the most important player. The quarterback."

"I see."

"Don't you like football, Miss Ramsey?" Trent inquired. He was a trifle piqued that she hadn't recognized him. Nor had she seemed suitably impressed to discover that she was sharing dinner with a man touted by some sportswriters as the finest quarterback in professional football since Starr and Staubach.

"I don't know very much about it, Mr. Gamblin. But I know more now than I did."

"How's that?"

"I know that the players go to summer camp."

His mouth split into a wide grin. Miss Ramsey had a sense of humor. The next few weeks might not be too taxing after all. In fact, he didn't remember when he'd enjoyed such a relaxing dinner. He didn't have to work at impressing his aunt. She already thought he hung the moon. Any charm he sent in Miss Ramsey's direction was equally certain to be appreciated. No effort was required there either. For the first time in years, he could be himself in the company of females, and it felt good.

"How is your shoulder, Trent?" Ruby turned to Rana to explain. "He has an injury that refuses to heal properly. A shoulder dislocation."

"Separation, Auntie."

"Sorry, a *separation*. His doctor recommended that he get away from his circle of friends and suspend his other activities so his shoulder would have the rest it needs to heal before training camp. Right, dear?"

"Right."

· · ·

It had been the right decision, he thought now as he leaned back and sipped the coffee Ruby had poured into his china cup. He probably did need the rest, the earlier hours, and regular meals that this sabbatical in Galveston promised. Aunt Ruby certainly wasn't boring. He still had fond memories of his childhood visits with her.

He looked speculatively at the other woman at the table. Miss Ramsey might even prove to be amusing, if she ever lightened up. Maybe he could prod her along.

"What do you do to support yourself?" he asked abruptly.

"Trent! How rude!" his aunt admonished. "Didn't that sister of mine teach you any social graces? You've been around those barbarian teammates of yours too long."

"I want to know." His smile was disarming. "Why beat around the bush? If Miss Ramsey and I are going to be . . . living together, don't you think we should get to know each other?"

His dark eyes had swept down Rana's body, leaving a tide of heat. Rana wished she hadn't felt it. For some unexplainable reason she had been relieved to learn that he wasn't seeking cover from a sticky divorce, though that didn't rule out the possibility that he was married.

She had even felt a twinge of pity for him as an athlete who was obviously worried about his future. She knew enough about the world of professional sports to know that such injuries as shoulder separations could mean the end of a career.

Now, however, when he was looking at her with that

familiar "I could eat you for breakfast, little girl" look on his face, her compassion evaporated and her previous aversion returned. With it came her resolution to keep out of his path.

"I paint," she said succinctly.

"Paint? You mean pictures or walls?"

"Neither." She sipped her coffee, creating what she hoped was an irritating delay. "I paint on clothing."

"Clothing?" he asked with a deadpan expression.

"Yes, clothing," she said, staring at him through the blue-tinted lenses of her glasses.

"She's ingenious," Ruby contributed with affected gaiety. She had so hoped her nephew could bring out Miss Ramsey, but during the course of this first meal, her hopes had been dashed. If anything, Miss Ramsey had retreated further into her shell. She seemed to be hiding behind her eyeglasses, shrinking inside her oversized ugly clothing, withdrawing even further behind a veil of secrecy and privacy. "You ought to see some of her creations," Ruby continued, undaunted. "She works too hard at it, though. I'm constantly after her to get out more. To mingle with people her own age."

Trent hadn't taken his eyes off Miss Ramsey. "You do your work here?"

"Yes. I've turned the sitting room of the apartment into a studio. The lighting is good."

"I'm not sure I understand." He stretched his long legs far out in front of him. His knee bumped into hers beneath the table; she quickly pulled hers back. "How do you paint on clothing? What kind of clothing? What do you use?"

She smiled, pleased with his interest in spite of herself. "I buy surplus garments and textiles in warehouses, then hand-paint original designs on them."

He scowled with skepticism. "There's a market for such, uh, clothes?"

"I can afford to pay my rent, Mr. Gamblin," she said tartly. She shoved back her chair abruptly and got to her feet. "It was a wonderful dinner, as usual, Ruby. Good night."

"You're not going to your room so early?" the landlady asked, distressed over Miss Ramsey's sudden mood swing. "I thought we all might have a cup of tea in the parlor."

"Excuse me tonight. I'm tired. Mr. Gamblin." She gave him a cool nod before stalking from the dining room.

"Well I'll be damned," Trent muttered. "What bee got up her—"

"Trent, don't be crude!" Ruby interrupted. "Wait! What are you— Where—"

Heedless of his aunt's surprised sputtering, he stood, tossed down his napkin, and left the table with the same angry urgency Miss Ramsey had displayed only seconds before. His long legs covered ground faster than she could. He caught up with her just as she reached the stairs. "Miss Ramsey!"

His voice carried with it the imperiousness of a drill sergeant. She stopped with her foot poised on the second step and turned around.

Before she could prevent it, he had her right hand firmly enfolded in his. "You didn't give me a chance to tell you how glad I am to find myself in your delightful company." Regardless of his seething anger, he spoke in dulcet tones. *No* woman walked out on Trent Gamblin. "*Enchanted,* Miss Ramsey." Lifting her hand, he pressed his mouth to the back of it.

She tried to hold in her gasp but failed. She felt as if she had been punched in the middle. Aftershocks rippled through her. Snatching her hand away from his, she spoke a frosty good night and haughtily retreated upstairs.

Trent was still smiling when he returned to the dining room. "I don't like the gloating expression on your face, Trent," Ruby said sternly.

He resumed his seat and poured himself another cup of coffee from the silver pot. "Miss Ramsey might act like a prickly old maid, but she's still a woman."

"I hope that you won't do anything indiscreet or treat Miss Ramsey with anything but the utmost respect. She is a dear girl, but treasures her privacy. In all these months, she hasn't divulged any personal information about herself. My guess is that there's a great sadness in her history. Please don't provoke her."

"I wouldn't think of it," he said with a smile that was anything but sincere.

Since his aunt had always adored him, she didn't question his earnestness. "Good. Now, be a sweetheart and come into the kitchen with me while I clean up. I want to hear everything that's been going on in your life."

"Even the raunchy stuff?"

She giggled and squeezed his chin between her fingers. "I want to hear the raunchy stuff first."

Trent followed his aunt into her kitchen, but his mind was still on Miss Ramsey. What the hell was her first name, anyway? He had noticed, in spite of her clothes—clothes that a bag lady would be ashamed to wear—that she had a remarkably graceful, fluid walk. Her posture was proud. The hand he had so arrogantly kissed might have been unmanicured, but it was dainty to the point of fragility. For some reason, despite the rough skin and the faint smell of paint and turpentine, he had enjoyed kissing it very much.